FIC
DUMAS

Chicago Public Library

R0406446151

HWLCFN

Sultanetta

C0-DXA-248

LITERATURE AND LANGUAGE DIVISION
THE CHICAGO PUBLIC LIBRARY
400 SOUTH STATE STREET
CHICAGO, ILLINOIS 60605

SULTANETTA

THE-ROMANCES-OF
AEXANDRE-DUMAS

Fredonia Books
Amsterdam, The Netherlands

Sultanetta

by
Alexandre Dumas

ISBN: 1-58963-756-9

Copyright © 2002 by Fredonia Books

Reprinted from the 1895 edition

Fredonia Books
Amsterdam, the Netherlands
http://www.fredoniabooks.com

All rights reserved, including the right to reproduce this book, or portions thereof, in any form.

In order to make original editions of historical works available to scholars at an economical price, this facsimile of the original edition of 1895 is reproduced from the best available copy and has been digitally enhanced to improve legibility, but the text remains unaltered to retain historical authenticity.

PREFACE.

One word as to the way in which the story I am about to relate fell into my hands.

I was at Derbend, the city of the Iron Gates, at the residence of the commander of the fortress. During breakfast the conversation turned on the novelist Marlinsky, who was no other than the Bestuchef that was condemned to the Siberian mines for the conspiracy of 1825, and whose brother was hanged at the citadel of St. Petersburg together with Pestel, Mouravief, Kalkovsky, and Ryleief.

Exempted from labor in the mines in 1827, Bestuchef had been sent as a soldier to the army of the Caucasus. Brave, and casting himself with desperation into every danger, he soon won the rank of ensign, and with this rank he lived a year in the fortress of Derbend.

You will read in my " Voyage au Caucase " what new catastrophe gave him a distaste for life, and how, in an encounter with the Lesghians, he met at their hands a death as voluntary as suicide.

Among the numerous papers left in his room at the time of his death, was found a manuscript. This manuscript has since been read by different persons, and among others by the commandant's daughter, who mentioned it

PREFACE.

to me as a novel of great interest. Upon her recommendation I had it translated, and finding, not only much of interest, as she had done, but also a very remarkable local coloring in the little romance, I determined to publish it.

I took it, consequently, from the hands of my translator; I rewrote it to render it comprehensible to French readers, and such as it is, without changing anything, I am publishing it, convinced that it will impress others in the same way that it has impressed me.

It is, moreover, a curious picture of war as carried on between the Russians, those representatives of the civilization of the North, and the wild, fierce tribes of the Caucasus.

ALEX. DUMAS.

SULTANETTA.

Period, 1819-1828.

ACKMETH, Khan of Avarie.
SULTANETTA, his daughter.
AMMALAT BEG, in love with Sultanetta.
SOPHYR ALI, his foster brother.
FATMA, an old Tartar woman, nurse of Ammalat Beg
DJEMBOULAT, a Kabardian prince.
COLONEL VERKOVSKY,
GENERAL YERMOLOF,
CAPTAIN BETOVITCH,
COLONEL KOTZAREV,
} Russian officers.
HADJI SOLEIMAN, a pious Turk.
NEPHTALI, a young Circassian.
ALIKPER, a blacksmith.

SULTANETTA.

I.

" Be slow to offend and quick to avenge." [1]

It was Friday.

Near Bouinaky, a large village of northern Daghestan, the Tartar youth had assembled for a horse-race, supplemented by every feat of hardihood and courage that could be annexed to this sort of fête.

Let us give some idea of the magnificent landscape in which the scene is enacted.

Bouinaky ascends the two spurs of a lofty mountain and commands the surrounding country. To the left of the road leading from Derbend to Tarky is outlined the crest of the Caucasus, covered with forests; on the right is the shore, against which the waters of the Caspian Sea beat with ceaseless murmur, or, rather, with ceaseless lamentation.

The day was fading.

The villagers, allured by the crispness of the air much more than by interest in a spectacle too often repeated to be novel, had left their huts, descended their mountain slopes and ranged themselves in rows on both sides of the road.

[1] Inscription engraved on the poniards of Daghestan.

As for the men, they stood in groups or squatted in Turkish fashion. Old men were smoking Persian tobacco in their Tchetchen pipes. The sound of hilarity prevailed over all, and mingling with the incessant uproar was heard from time to time the clashing of a horse's hoofs against the flints of the road, and the cry of "*Katch! katch!*" ("Clear the way! clear the way!") uttered by the riders making ready for the race.

Nature is radiant in Daghestan during the month of May; thousands of roses cover the granite with the ruddy tint of dawn, and the air is redolent of their perfume; the nightingales, deep in the green twilights of the groves, are perpetually singing. Bounding over the rocks are flocks of sportive sheep, embellished with orange-colored spots which the shepherds, full of whimsical fancies with regard to them, make with henna, the same material that their masters employ in staining the nails of the hands and feet. Buffaloes, plunged in the marshes in voluptuous enjoyment, gaze at the passer-by with great profound eyes which would seem menacing were they not pensive. The steppes are covered with heather of many hues. Every wave of the Caspian glistens like the scaly coat of a giant fish. With every breath, in short, quickening the senses and gladdening the heart, is inhaled something of that seductiveness of air, of sky, of atmosphere, which inspired in the Greeks the instinctive divination that the world was born here, that the Caucasus was its cradle.

Such is the impression that native or foreigner would have received on nearing the village of Bouinaky that jocund Friday, the birthday of the events we are about to chronicle.

The sun was gilding the sombre walls of the flat-roofed houses, whose shadows gathered the greater depth and

SULTANETTA. 3

strength the farther he withdrew. At a distance could be heard the doleful creaking of the *arabas* [1] of which a long line was distinguishable among the Tartar rocks that stood like ghosts in a graveyard, and in the lead of their noisy procession galloped a horseman raising a cloud of dust upon the road.

The snowy crest of the mountains, and the calm sea opposite, invested the scene with a vast magnificence.

One felt that Nature was alive with the keenest, most ardent spirit.

"It is he! it is he! he is coming! there he is!" cried the throng at sight of this dust and the horseman it screened from view, but whose identity they already guessed.

At these cries there was great commotion among the crowd.

Horsemen who had been standing about until then with their bridles over their arms, talking with acquaintances, leaped upon their horses; those who had been galloping right and left at random and according to their whim drew together, and all hastened away to meet this horseman and his suite.

It was Ammalat Beg, nephew of the Chamkal [2] Tarkovsky.

He wore a black tchouska of Persian make, trimmed with the exquisite galoons whose secret only Caucasian manufacturers possess; the sleeves, half hanging, were caught up by the ends to the shoulder. His arkalouke of tarmalama was confined to the figure by a Turkish scarf:

---

[1] The *arabas* are carts whose wheels, never being greased, on account of their proprietors' repugnance to pork, at every revolution emit a groan that can be compared to nothing but that of the Spanish *norias*.

[2] A Tartar title equivalent to the Russian *kness*, prince.

his red trousers were lost in yellow boots, with high heels; his gun, poniard, and pistols were mounted in silver embossed with gold; his sword-hilt was adorned with precious stones. Added to this, the heir of Chamkal Tarkovsky was twenty-four years old, handsome, well made, and of an open countenance; add, too, that long ringlets of black hair fell from his papak on his neck, that a little black moustache which seemed traced by a pencil adorned his lips, that his eyes glowed with haughty kindliness, that he was mounted on a black charger always ready to run, that he was seated on a light, silver-embroidered, Circassian saddle, that his feet rested in black Khorassan stirrups of steel embossed with gold, that twenty noukars in embroidered tchouskas galloped at his side on splendid horses, and you will realize the impression created by the arrival of the young prince in the midst of a people upon whom wealth, grace, beauty, the external endowments, in short, which Oriental skies lavish upon its elect, have such supreme influence and for whom they have such irresistible attraction.

The men stood up and saluted him, bowing with hands upon hearts.

Murmurs of delight, of awe, and especially of admiration, rose from among the women.

Reaching the centre of the crowd, Ammalat Beg stopped.

The old men, leaning on their staffs, and the leading citizens of Bouinaky gathered round him, hoping the young beg would speak to them; but the young beg did not even look their way.

Instead, he raised his hand for the race to begin.

Without other orders, a score of riders then dashed off at a gallop, each striving to outdistance his neighbor.

Then they all seized their djerids, or javelins, and hurled them at each other at full speed.

The most skilful ones picked them up again without setting foot to earth, while swinging down and under their horses' stomachs.

Others, less skilled, trying to imitate them, rolled in the dust amid shouts of laughter from the by-standers.

The shooting began.

Thus far during the race Ammalat Beg had held aloof; but his noukars had one after another allowed themselves to be drawn away and were mingling with the competitors.

Only two remained with the prince.

But, with the excitement of the races, the echoing shots, and the pungent smell of powder-smoke filling the air, the young chamkal's icy indifference seemed to thaw. He began to shout at the combatants, rising in his stirrups to urge them on, and, when his favorite noukar's ball missed the papak that he had thrown into the air in front of him, he could no longer restrain himself, but seized his gun and dashed at full gallop into the midst of the marksmen.

"Make way for Ammalat Beg!" was heard on all sides.

And they moved aside as quickly as if the warning had been: "Way for the waterspout! Way for the hurricane!"

Along a verst's distance ten poles had been erected, a papak crowning each.

Ammalat Beg set his horse at a gallop, rode past them from first to last, his gun held high above his head; then when he had passed the last, he turned again, and rising in his stirrups, fired without a halt.

The papak fell.

Then, still galloping, he reloaded his gun, retraced his course, returning the same way that he had come, dropped the second papak in like manner, and so on to the last of the ten.

This display of skill, ten times repeated, elicited universal applause.

Ammalat Beg did not pause; once aroused, his pride demanded a complete triumph. He tossed away his gun. took his pistol, whirled in his saddle so as to ride backward, and, as the horse threw up his hind feet in the gallop, he fired and unshod the right foot; then, reloading, he did the same with the left foot.

There were shouts of admiration.

Next, picking up his gun, he ordered one of his noukars to gallop ahead of him.

The two set off, swift as thought.

In mid-career, the noukar threw a silver rouble high into the air.

Amalat Beg brought his gun to his shoulder, but at that instant his horse stumbled and rolled over, ploughing the dust of the road with his head.

A single cry was heard; it had issued simultaneously from all throats.

But the skilled horseman remained standing in the stirrups, no more disconcerted than if nothing had happened, and, just as his two feet were touching the earth, he fired.

The rouble, driven by the ball, fell far outside of the assemblage of people.

The crowd, intoxicated with delight, burst into frantic hurrahs.

But Ammalat Beg, calm, and to all appearance, unmoved, quickly disengaged his feet from the stirrups, aided his horse to rise, and threw the rein to one of his noukars to have him instantly shod.

The racing and shooting continued.

Just then the foster-brother of Ammalat Beg, Sophyr Ali, the son of a poor beg of Bouinaky, approached.

He was a handsome youth, simple-hearted and happy; he had been raised and had grown to manhood by the side of Ammalat. The same intimacy existed between them as between two brothers.

He jumped down from his horse, bowed, and said, —

"The noukar Mohammed is tiring out your old horse Antrim, trying to make him leap a ravine over fifteen feet wide."

"And does n't Antrim take it?" cried Ammalat, frowning with annoyance. "Bring him to me at once."

He went to meet the horse, made a sign for the noukar to dismount, vaulted into the saddle, and directed Antrim straight to the ditch to make him look at it.

Then, retracing his steps, he started from the field at full gallop towards the ravine.

The nearer he approached, the harder he pressed with his knees and drew on the bridle.

But, not having confidence in his strength, Antrim swerved to the right with a sudden dash.

Ammalat Beg rode back into the field and again he set off at full speed.

This time, stimulated by the whip, Antrim rose to his hind feet as if about to make the leap.

But instead of taking the ditch, he turned on his hind feet as on a pivot, and refused it a second time.

Ammalat Beg was furious.

In vain did Sophyr Ali beg him not to urge the poor beast that had so honorably spent his powers in races and battles; Ammalat paid no heed, and, drawing his schaska from its sheath, he forced him to make a third attempt, rousing him this time not only with the whip but with the blade of his sword.

But it was of no avail; as twice before, the horse stopped at the edge of the ditch.

But this time Ammalat Beg gave poor Antrim such a blow between the ears with his schaska, that the horse dropped like a felled ox.

Ammalat Beg had killed him at one stroke.

"That is a faithful servant's reward!" remarked Sophyr Ali, with a sigh, looking sadly at the dead animal.

"No, it is punishment for disobedience," angrily retorted Ammalat Beg.

Sophyr Ali was silent.

The horsemen continued riding.

Suddenly there was a sound of beating drums, and, rising gradually from behind the mountains, the glittering points of Russian bayonets could be seen.

It was a company of Kousinsk's regiment on their return from escorting a wheat-train to Derbend.

The captain commanding this company marched with another officer a little in advance of the troop.

Thinking it time for his men to rest, the captain ordered a halt.

They stacked their arms, left a sentinel in charge, and stretched themselves on the grass.

The arrival of a detachment of Russians was no novelty to the people of Bouinaky in 1819; but such a sight is not a very agreeable one, even to-day, to the men of Daghestan. Their religion causes them to regard the Russians as their undying enemies, and if they sometimes smile upon them, it is to conceal their real feelings behind the smile; and the real feelings are of hatred, implacable and deadly.

A murmur passed through the crowd as the Russians halted on their race-course. The women regained their houses, not however without a glance at the new-comers through the openings of their veils; the men, on the contrary, eyed them askance, gathering in groups and speaking in low tones.

But the older men, more prudent, approached the captain and asked after his health.

"I myself am very well," said he; "but my horse has cast a shoe, so that he limps. Fortunately, here is a good Tartar," he continued, pointing to the smith that was shoeing Ammalat's horse, "who will remedy the matter."

Then, approaching him, he said, —

"Eh! friend, when you have finished putting a new sole on the horse you are working at, you shall do as much for mine."

The smith, whose face was doubly blackened by sun and soot, turned a glowering look upon the captain, twisted his moustache, crushed his papak down to his ears, but made no reply; and when he had done with Ammalat Beg's horse, he tranquilly replaced his instruments in his sack.

"Ah! see here! did you understand me?" demanded the captain.

"Perfectly," retorted the smith.

"What did I say, then?"

"That your horse had cast a shoe."

"Well, since you understand, set yourself to work."

"To-day is Friday, it is a holiday; no one works on holidays."

"Listen," said the captain, "I will pay whatever you ask; but understand one thing, — if you will not do it of your own accord, you shall be made to do it."

"Before all other commands I must obey Allah's, who forbids me to work on Friday. I already sin too much on ordinary days, but I will think twice on a day like this! I am not anxious to buy my own coal to burn me in hell."

"Then what were you doing just now?" insisted the captain, beginning in turn to knit his brows. "Were you not at work? It strikes me that a horse is a horse, especially mine; he is a pure blooded Mussulman. Look, don't you recognize him for a Karabach?"

"A horse is a horse, it is true, and there is no difference between them when they are of good blood; but it is not so with men. The horse that I have just shod is Ammalat Beg's and Ammalat Beg is my chief."

"Which is saying that if you had not obeyed him, he would have cut off your two ears, you knave! and because you do not grant me the right to do as much, you will not work for me. Very well, my man! I'll not cut off your ears, because the thing is forbidden to us Christians; but you can be sure of getting two hundred lashes on your back if you don't obey me. Do you hear?"

"I hear."

"Well?"

"Well, as I am a good Mussulman, my second answer shall be the same as my first: to-day is Friday, and Mussulmans do not work on Fridays."

"You think so?"

"I am sure of it."

"Since you worked for your Tartar chief's pleasure, you shall work for a Russian officer's necessity. I say necessity, because if my horse is not shod I cannot continue my journey. — Here, soldiers!"

Already a large group had collected round the two disputants; but it became suddenly greater and more crowded at this point in the quarrel, and voices from among the Tartars were heard: —

"No, that must not be; it cannot be permitted. This is Friday; no one works on Fridays."

At the same time many of the blacksmith's friends began to cram their papaks down over their eyes and grasp the hilts of their poniards, crowding upon the captain and shouting to the smith, —

"Don't you shoe the Russian's horse, Alikper, don't you touch his beast; what you do for Ammalat Beg, a good Mussulman, you need not do for a dog of a Muscovite."

The captain was brave; besides, he knew the Asiatics.

"Clear out, you rabble!" he cried, drawing a pistol from its holster; "or, if you stay, hold your tongues! for, as sure as that you will all be damned, the first one who says a word will get his lips sealed with lead."

This threat, backed by the bayonets of numerous soldiers, had its effect. The cowards disappeared, the courageous stood their ground, though without saying another word.

As for Master Alikper, seeing that matters looked serious for him, he cast about for some way of escape, and perceiving none, he muttered a few words in Turk which evidently framed an excuse to the Prophet, rolled up his sleeves, opened his sack, extracted his hammer and chisel, and proceeded to obey.

It should be added that Ammalat Beg knew nothing of what was passing. As soon as he saw the Russians, not desiring a disagreeable encounter with them, he addressed a few words to an old woman, his nurse, who had watched him with maternal affection throughout all the feats of skill which he had just executed, and leaping upon his horse he took the road to his own house which, like an eagle's eyrie, overhung the village of Bouinaky.

But, although one of the important characters in our story was just departing in one direction, another character, also important to a certain degree, was at the same moment approaching from the opposite one.

II.

This was a cavalier low of stature but strongly built. He seemed to belong to the easily recognized tribe of the Avares: he wore a helmet and breastplate of chain armor, carried a small shield in his left hand, and a straight-bladed schaska hung from his side.

The only thing lacking in the new arrival's costume, a costume which is to-day exactly the same as was that of the Crusaders, was the cross of red cloth worn on the right breast by those mountaineers who had remained faithful to the Christain religion.

The others, becoming converts to the Moslem religion, from either necessity or conviction, retain the same costume but without the sign of our redemption.

This horseman was accompanied. by five noukars,[1] thoroughly equipped like himself.

From the dusty covering of the riders and the foaming flanks of their horses, it was easy to surmise that they had made a long and rapid journey.

As the head horseman, whom we have accorded particular mention, was leisurely passing the Russian soldiers, to whom he seemed insolently indifferent, he passed their guns so closely as to graze one of the stands of arms and knock it down.

But without appearing to remark the incident, he continued on his way, while his noukars carelessly allowed their horses to trample the overturned guns.

[1] Noukars are squires or equerries to be found in the suite of every noble Tartar.

The sentinel, who from a distance had warned the horseman, "Keep off!" — an injunction which it is seen had produced no great effect, — sprang to his horse's bridle, while the soldiers, considering themselves insulted by the contemptuous behavior of the Mussulmans, began to mutter threateningly among themselves.

"Who are you?" cried the sentinel, seizing, as we have said, the bridle of the chief of this little band.

"You are new to the country, if you have not recognized Ackmeth, khan of Avarie," composedly responded the horseman, snatching his horse's bridle from the sentinel's hand. "It seems to me, however, that a year ago, near Backli, I made a deep impression on the Russians."

Then, as he had spoken in Tartar, turning to one of his noukars, he added, —

"Tell these dogs in their own language what I have just done them the honor to say."

The noukar repeated in Russian, word for word, what Ackmeth Khan had just said in Tartar.

"It is Ackmeth Khan! it is Ackmeth Khan!" repeated the soldiers in chorus. "Seize him! Don't let him escape, now that we have him! We must be avenged for the Backli affair!"

"Back, wretches!" yelled Ackmeth Khan, fetching the sentinel's hand a blow with his whip. "Have you forgotten that I am to-day a Russian general?"

And this time he spoke in such pure Muscovite that the soldiers lost not a word of it.

"A Russian traitor, you mean!" cried several of the soldiers. "Let us take him to the captain, or to Derbend, to Colonel Verkovsky."

"Only to hell would I go with such an escort," sneered Ackmeth Khan.

At the same time he made his horse rear to his hind feet, swayed him to the right, then to the left, and at last, striking his hind-quarters a violent blow with his whip, he leaped him over the sentinel, who was overthrown by the shock.

The noukars set their horses at a gallop and followed their khan, who rode about a hundred paces at full speed and then allowed his horse to resume his ordinary gait, all the while indifferently trifling with his bridle.

Then only was his attention attracted by the crowd of Tartars gathered about the farrier, who had begun to shoe the captain's horse; for, just as the captain had failed to see what was taking place behind his back, so had Ackmeth Khan been in ignorance of what was going on ahead of him.

"Is there any disturbance here?" inquired the khan, pulling up his horse. "What is the trouble? what is the dispute about?"

"Ah! the khan!" cried the Tartars.

And they bowed respectfully.

Ackmeth Khan repeated his question.

They related the affair of the captain and the farrier.

"And you stand looking on, as unmoved and stupid as buffaloes, while your brother is being outraged, your customs are set at naught, and your religion is trampled under foot!" cried Ackmeth Khan; "and you mumble like so many old women, instead of taking your revenge! Why don't you weep?"

Then three times in tones of deepest scorn he exclaimed, —

"Cowards! cowards! cowards!"

"And what can we do?" returned several voices. "The Russians have muskets and bayonets."

"And you, have you no guns and poniards? Shame!

shame to the Mussulmans! The sword of Daghestan to cower under the Muscovite whip!"

Eyes flashed.

Ackmeth continued: —

"Ah! you fear muskets and bayonets, but you do not fear dishonor. Between hell and Siberia, you choose hell. Did your ancestors behave in that way? Did your fathers think as you do? They did not count the enemy, but whatever their number, they rushed upon them shouting, 'Allah!' and if they fell, they at least fell with glory. Are the Russians, perchance, of better mettle than you? Have their guns never turned but their muzzles upon you? A bull is to be taken by the horns, wretches! A scorpion is seized by the tail, cowards!"

And as before, he three times ejaculated, —

"Cowards! cowards! cowards!"

This time the insult struck the Tartars full in the breast.

"He is right!" they cried; "Ackmeth Khan is rigth! We are too strong to take all that from the Russians. Free the farrier! free Alikper!"

And, more menacing than ever, they began to crowd upon the soldiers in whose centre the smith was shoeing the captain's horse.

The revolt was growing.

Satisfied with having brought matters to this pass, and not wishing to compromise himself in such a small affair, Achmeth Khan left two of his noukars to egg on the Tartars, and followed by the other three, he pursued up the mountain the shortest route leading to the home of Ammalat Beg.

The latter had already regained his house, and he was lying upon a divan smoking his khalian.

On seeing Ackmeth Khan appear at his threshold, he rose and went to meet him.

"May you conquer!" said Ackmeth Khan to Ammalat Beg.

This Circassian greeting was uttered with so much significance that Ammalat Beg, after embracing Ackmeth Khan, inquired, —

"Were you jesting or prophesying when you addressed me just now, my dear guest?"

"That depends on you, and will be as you please. The heir of Tarkovsky's principality has only to draw his sword — "

"Never to sheath it again, khan!"

Then, shaking his head, he continued, —

"It would be a bad thing for me. It is much better to be the quiet and undisputed lord of Bouinaky than to be hiding in the mountains like an outlaw."

"Or like a lion, Ammalat. Lions, too, live in the mountains to be free."

The young man sighed.

"It is much better to dream on without waking, Ackmeth, — I am asleep, do not wake me."

"It is the Russians who are administering the opium that puts you to sleep; and, in your lethargy, another culls the golden fruits of your garden."

"What can I do with the small force that I have?"

"Force lies in the soul, Ammalat. Do but dare, and everything will give way before you."

Then, assuming a listening attitude, he added, —

"Hark! there's another voice besides mine calling on you to arouse yourself; it is victory's!"

In fact, the sound of a lively fusillade reached the ears of the two princes.

At that moment Sophyr Ali entered the room, his face pale and agitated.

"Do you hear, chamkal?" said he. "Bouinaky is in

revolt. A mob has surrounded the company of Russians and the Tartars are firing on the soldiers."

"Ah! the rascals!" cried Ammalat Beg, springing for his gun. "How have they dared do such a thing without me? Run on, Sophyr Ali; command them in my name to keep quiet, and kill the first who disobeys."

"I tried to quiet them," answered the young man; "but they would not listen. Ackmeth Khan's noukars are there urging them on, shouting, 'Kill the Russians!'"

"Did my noukars really shout that?" asked Ackmeth Khan, with a smile.

"They not only shouted that, but they set the example by shooting first," said Sophyr Ali.

"In that case," remarked Ackmeth Khan, "they are brave men, and they can take a hint when it is given to them."

"What have you done, Ackmeth Khan?" remonstrated Ammalat Beg, sorrowfully.

"What you should have done long ago."

"How shall I face the Russians now?"

"With ball and kandjiar. Fate is at work for you, happy rebel. Come, out with our schaskas and let us fall upon the Russians!"

"Here they are!" thundered the captain, bursting into the room with two men, so rapidly had he climbed the mountain slope which led to Ammalat's house.

Then, turning to his two men, he said, —

"Guard the doors, there, and see that no one goes out.'

The soldiers obeyed.

Annoyed at this unexpected revolt in which he could very easily be implicated, although he had not taken the slightest hand in it, Ammalat advanced to the captain and in a friendly tone, contrasting with the angry accents of the other, he inquired in Tartar speech, —

"Do you bring peace into my house, brother?"

"I do not know what I am bringing into your house, Ammalat," said the captain; "but I do know the kind of reception I am getting in your village; I am received as an enemy, and your men have fired on the soldiers of my — your — of our common emperor."

They have done wrong to fire on the Russians," interposed Ackmeth Khan reclining indolently among the cushions of the divan and drawing a whiff at the khalian abandoned by Ammalat Beg; "they have not done well, unless every shot has killed its man."

"See, there lies the cause of all the mischief, Ammalat!" cried the captain angrily, pointing at Ackmeth Khan. "But for him everything would be quiet in Bouinaky. Really, you are a fine one, Ammalat. You call yourself the friend of the Russians, and receive their enemy as your guest! You conceal him like an accomplice! Ammalat Beg, in the name of the emperor, I demand that you deliver up this man to me."

"Captain," replied Ammalat gently but firmly, "you know that with us a guest is sacred. It would be criminal in me to deliver up my guest. Do not insist; have some regard for our customs, and, if I must say it, for my entreaty."

"And I say, Ammalat, duty before custom; hospitality is sacred, but the oath is still more sacred. The oath forbids our defrauding justice of even our own brother, if that brother is a criminal."

"I would sooner betray my brother than my guest, captain. Besides, it is not for you to dictate to me what course I shall follow. If I sin, Allah and the padishah will judge me. Let the Prophet guard the khan on mountain or plain: once there, I have nothing to say; but here, under my own roof, it is my duty to defend him," and, added the young prince resolutely, "I shall defend him."

"Then you countenance a traitor?" the captain asked.

Ackmeth Khan had taken no part in the controversy; he smoked his khalian as placidly as if some other person were in question; but at the word *traitor*, he bounded rather than rose to his feet, and approaching the captain he said, —

"You call me a traitor; say rather that I might have been a traitor to those to whom I should be faithful. The Russian padishah bestowed power on me, and I was grateful to him as long as he did not demand the impossible. I was desired to admit the Russian troops into Avaria, to permit them to build fortresses there. What would you have called me then, had I betrayed the blood and the liberties of those over whom Allah had set me as father and chief? But, had I so wished, I could not have succeeded; thousands of poniards would have pierced my heart; the rocks would have wrenched themselves from their places and fallen upon my head. I held myself aloof from the friendship of the Russians, but I was not yet their enemy. What reward had I for my forbearance? I was insulted by a letter from one of your generals. He paid dearly for that insult at Backli. For a few words, I spilled a river of blood, and that river of blood separates you and me forever."

"And that blood cries for vengeance!" yelled the infuriated captain; "vengeance which you shall not escape. miscreant!"

And he moved as if to seize Ackmeth Khan by the throat.

But before his hand could touch the mountain chieftain, the latter's kandjiar was buried deep in his vitals

SULTANETTA.

Without uttering a syllable, without breathing a sigh, the captain fell dead on the carpet.

Then, drawing his pistol from his belt with the same rapidity and snatching Ammalat Beg's from his, Ackmeth Khan, with two shots as swift as a flash, as deadly as lightning, laid at his feet the two Russians who were guarding the door.

Ammalat Beg saw him do it without having time to avert this threefold murder.

"You have ruined me, Ackmeth," said he, mournfully. "That man was a Russian and he was my guest."

"There are some offences that the roof does not cover, chamkal," said the khan; "but this is no time for argument: let us shut the doors, summon your men and march upon the enemy."

"An hour ago they were not my enemies," said Ammalat Beg, "and now how would you have me march against them? I have no powder, I have no balls, and my men are scattered."

"The Russians! the Russians!" cried Sophyr Ali, rushing in, and paling with horror at sight of the three bodies.

"Come with me, Ammalat," said the khan. "I was going into Tchetchina to arouse them over the border; what will come of it, God knows! But there is bread and water in the mountains, and powder and shot. That is all a mountaineer needs. What say you?"

"Let us be off, then," answered Ammalat, his decision made. "Nothing but flight is left for me. You are right, it is no time for recrimination and reproach. My horse and six noukars to go with me, Sophyr Ali, —"

"And I, and I, too?" said the young man, interrupting him with tears in his eyes.

"No. You, my dear Sophyr, must remain here to

watch that the house is not plundered. Convey my salutations to my wife and take her to her father's. Do not forget me. Farewell!"

And, as Ackmeth Khan and Ammalat went out at one door. the Russians came in at another.

III

A SULTRY noon of spring hung over the Caucasus.

The muèzzins' voices were calling the people of Tchetchina to prayer, and their droning monotones, after having awakened for an instant an echo in the rocks, little by little died away on the still air.

The mullah, Hadji Soleiman, a pious Turk, sent into the mountains by the divan of Stamboul to strengthen the faith of the mountaineers and at the same time to incite them to revolt against the Russians, was reposing on the roof of the mosque, having performed his ablutions and prayers. Only a short time prior to this, he had been appointed mullah of the village of the Tchetchen Igalis, and this, without doubt, was the reason why he so solemnly contemplated his beard, and so seriously watched the wreaths of smoke curling from his chibouk.

Moreover, from time to time his eye dwelt with satisfaction on the black mouths of two or three caves hollowed out of the rock just in front of him.

At his left rose the crests of the range separating Tchetchina from Avarie, and beyond them towered the snowy peaks of the Caucasus. The cottages scattered over the slopes descended in cascade-like groups half-way down the mountain-side, where they stopped, forming a fortress accessible only by narrow paths, and, created by nature, providing the mountaineers with an ark of safety for their liberties.

All was quiet within the village and on the neighboring mountains; not a soul was to be seen on highway or by-way. Flocks of sheep had sought the shade of the ravines; buffaloes were huddled together in a narrow muddy stream, and, embedded in its mire, only their heads were exhibited above the water. The faint buzzing of insects, the monotonous chirp of the cricket, were the only signs of life that nature submitted amid the mournful stillness of the mountains, and, lying under the cupola, Hadji Soleiman was admiring, with the calm pertaining only to a reposeful people, that inert splendor of nature, so harmonious with the indolence of the Mussulman. He was all but closing his eyes, in whose wavering sight the fire and light of the sun seemed to have been extinguished, when, through that blurred vision, he became conscious of two horsemen who were clambering slowly up the mountain opposite the one with the hollow caverns.

"Nephtali!" called the mullah, turning toward the cottage nearest the mosque, and before whose door was a saddled horse.

At this call, a handsome Circassian, his beard short without being shaved, his head covered by a papak that concealed half of his face, appeared in the street.

"I see two horsemen," continued the mullah; "and they are skirting the village."

"They are Jews or Armenians," answered Nephtali. "For economy's sake they have not been willing to hire a guide, and they will break their necks on the path which they have undertaken; none but wild goats and Tchetchina's best riders follow that trail."

"No, brother Nephtali," said the mullah. "I have made two trips to Mecca, and I know Jews and Armenians perfectly well. These horsemen are neither the one nor the other. If they were Jews or Armenians, they would be coming on commercial business, and would have baggage; but, do you look, — your eyes are young and, consequently, keener than mine. I could once," continued the mullah, "at a verst's distance have counted the buttons on a Russian soldier's uniform, and the ball that I aimed at the infidel never missed its mark; but to-day, at the same distance, I can hardly tell a buffalo from a horse."

And he heaved a sigh.

While he was speaking, rather to himself than to his companion, the latter had quickly ascended to him, and was scanning the travellers, who continued to approach.

"The day is warm, and travel is fatiguing," said the mullah; "invite these two travellers to refresh themselves and rest their horses. Perhaps they have some news. The Koran tells us to welcome the wayfarers."

"Even before the Koran had penetrated our mountains," said Nephtali, "never did a traveller leave the village without resting in it and receiving refreshment; never did he say good-by without a blessing, or set out without a guide for the rest of his journey; yet I feel suspicious of these travellers. Why do they avoid friendly people? and, instead of going through the hamlet, why do they pass at one side at the risk of their lives?"

"At any rate, they seem to me to be compatriots," said Hadji Soleiman, shading his eyes with his hand to ward off the sun's rays. "They wear the Tchetchen garb; perhaps, again, these are the two brothers bound by an oath to avenge blood by blood."

"No, Soleiman," said the young man, shaking his head; "no, these men are none of ours. No mountaineer would come here expressly to boast of a fight with the Russians and to show their weapons. Neither are they *abrecks;*[1] the *abrecks*, were they passing through a village of their bitterest enemies, would not draw their bachliks[2] over their faces. The garb sometimes deceives, hadji; who knows but what these are Russian deserters? Not long ago a Cossack escaped from the hamlet of Goumbet after killing the master of the house where he lived, and stealing his horse and weapons. The devil is very crafty, and often the strongest will yield to temptation."

"There is no strength where the faith is weak, Nephtali; but stay, I see curls below the papak of the second horseman."

"May I be ground to powder if it is not so!" exclaimed Nephtali. "He is a Russian, or, worse still, a Shiite Tartar.[3] Wait, wait, I will frizzle his curly locks for him. I shall return in half an hour, Soleiman. In half an hour they shall either be our guests, or one of us shall measure the height of the precipice."

Nephtali quickly descended the stairs, took his gun, sprang to horse, and dashed off at full gallop over the mountain, unmindful alike of rocks and ravines. But in the distance the stones could be seen flying like dust behind this daring rider.

"*Allah akbar!*" said the hadji proudly, as he relighted his extinguished chibook.

Nephtali soon overtook the two riders. Their horses, jaded, and covered with foam, were raining sweat upon the narrow path along which they were toiling up the mountain. One rider wore the Tchepsour's coat of mail,

---

[1] The *abrecks* are mountaineers who have taken oath to court peril, and who consequently use no precaution to avoid it.

[2] Hoods.

[3] Mussulmans are divided into two hostile sects, — Sunnites and Shiites; Nephtali and Soleiman are Sunnites.

the other, the Circassian costume; only, at variance with this costume, a Persian sabre instead of a schaska was suspended from the rich girdle wound around his person.

Their faces could not be seen, their bachliks being drawn down; perhaps they desired protection from the sun, perhaps they did not desire to be recognized

Nephtali followed behind them along the narrow path on the verge of the precipice; but, the path becoming a little wider, he went ahead and barred the way.

"*Salaam aleikoum!*" said he, resting his loaded gun across the saddle.

The first of the two strangers raised his bachlik, but only enough to see without being seen.

"*Aleikoum salaam!*" he responded, detaching his gun and rising in the stirrups.

"God grant you safe conduct!" continued Nephtali, getting ready to slay, at the first hostile movement, the traveller for whom he asked God's protection.

"As for you," answered the unknown in the coat of mail, "God grant you enough intelligence to keep you from barricading a traveller's path another time. What do you want, *kounack?*"[1]

"To proffer rest and refreshment for yourselves, and a stable for your horses. There is ever room in my house for guests. The wayfarer's blessing multiplies the flocks. Cast not upon our village the reproach that any have passed without stopping."

"Thanks, brother. We have not come into the mountains to visit; we are in haste."

"Be warned!" replied Nephtali; "you ride to meet danger unless you take a guide."

"A guide?" repeated the traveller, with a laugh; "a guide in the Caucasus? Why, I know the mountain

[1] Brother. comrade.

much better than any of you; I have been where jaguars have not, where serpents never crawl, where none but eagles perch. Stand aside, comrade; your house is not on my way, and I have no time to lose prating with you."

"I will not yield an inch," answered the young man, "until I know your name."

"Thank your stars, Nephtali, that I knew your father; I have often ridden to battle by his side. But, out of my path, or, in spite of the friendship I bear her, your mother shall weep to-morrow at sight of shreds of her son's flesh in the teeth of jackals and the beaks of eagles. Unworthy son, you are coursing the highways, seeking quarrels with travellers, while your father's bones are bleaching on the Russian plain and the Cossack women are selling his weapons! Nephtali, your father was killed yesterday on the other side of the Terek. Now, since you wish to know who I am, look at me."

"Sultan Ackmeth Khan!" exclaimed the young Tchetchen, doubly agitated by the tidings he had just received and the severity of the traveller's regard.

"Yes, I am Ackmeth Khan," replied the prince; "but bear in mind, Nephtali, that if you say to any one, 'I have seen the khan of Avarie,' my vengeance shall pursue your descendants even to the last generation."

The young man stood respectfully aside, and the travellers passed him by.

Ackmeth Khan again relapsed into the silence from which the young man's intrusion had aroused him. He was plunged in sad reflections. The second traveller, Ammalat Beg, — for it was he, — like the khan, was pensive and silent. Their clothes bore traces of a recent fight, their mustaches were powder-singed, and smears of blood had dried on their faces. But Ackmeth Khan's proud bearing seemed to challenge all nature; a scornful smile played on his lips.

As for Ammalat Beg, his features wore a jaded look of fatigue. He scarcely glanced about him; but from time to time a sigh escaped his lips, wrested from him by the pain of a wounded hand.

The gait of his horse, little used to the mountains, fretted as much as it wearied him.

He was the first to break silence.

"Why did you refuse the invitation of that kind young man?" he demanded of the khan of Avarie. "We could have stopped an hour or two."

"You think and talk like a child, my dear Ammalat," returned the khan. "You are accustomed to governing Tartars and ordering them about like slaves, and you think the same course can be pursued with the mountaineers. The hand of fate lies heavy on us; we are beaten and pursued; more than a hundred mountaineers, your noukars and mine, have fallen by Russian balls. Would you that we show the Tchetchens the vanquished Ackmeth Khan, whom they are wont to look upon as the star of victory? Shall I appear before them as an outlaw? Shall I confess my own shame? To accept a needed hospitality, to submit myself to reproaches for the deaths of husbands and sons drawn by me into this engagement, is to lose their confidence. In time, their tears will dry; then Ackmeth Khan will reappear before them, the prophet of pillage and blood, and I will then lead them again to battle on the Russian frontiers. Were the desperate Tchetchens to catch sight of me to-day, they would not recollect that Allah alone dispenses and withholds victory. They might insult me with some imprudent speech, and I have never forgiven an insult; in that case, a petty personal vengeance might thrust itself across my path on some day when I am setting out against the ranks of the Russians. Why should I quarrel unnecessarily with a brave people? Why should I myself prostrate the idol of glory upon which they are accustomed to gaze with dazzled eyes? If I descend to the common ranks, every man will begin to measure his shoulder by mine. As for you, you are in need of a physician, and you will find none better than mine. To-morrow we shall be at home; keep up your courage till then."

Ammalat Beg carried his hand in graceful acknowledgment to heart and brow; he recognized the force of the khan's words, but he was weak from loss of blood.

Continuing to avoid the villages, they spent the night among the Tartar rocks, eating a little rice and honey, — provisions without which a mountaineer never undertakes a journey, however short it may be. They crossed the Koissu by the bridge near Scherté. They left behind them Andi, Boulins, and the ridge of the Salatahur. Their way lay through forests and along precipices appalling to both sight and soul. At last they began to ascend the range that separated them on the north from Khunsack, the capital of the khan. To reach the summit of this ridge, the travellers were obliged to pursue diagonal paths, continually doubling on their tracks, but at each step gaining somewhat on the height. The khan's horse, born to the mountains and accustomed to these arduous trails, stepped cautiously; but Ammalat Beg's young and spirited charger kept stumbling and falling at every step. His master's favorite, and pampered by him, he was unequal to such a forced march in the mountains. Under a blazing sun, amidst fields of snow, he could scarcely gasp, and with violent effort his dilated nostrils appeared to breathe fire, while the foam tossed from his bit.

"*Allah bereket!* "[1] cried Ammalat Beg, as they attained the culminating point of the mountain, whence his gaze embraced the whole of Avarie.

But, at the same instant, his horse sank under him; the blood gushed from the noble animal's mouth, and his last sigh burst the girth.

The khan assisted Ammalat Beg to free himself from his stirrups; but he saw with dismay that, in his fall, the young man's handkerchief had slipped from the wound, and the blood which they had with such difficulty stanched was flowing afresh.

But this time Ammalat was unconscious of his pain; he was weeping over his dead horse.

A drop is enough to overflow the full cup.

"Never again will you carry me like a feather in the wind, my brave charger," said he; "nor in a cloud of dust in the race while I hear the shouts of those left behind me, nor amidst cheering warriors through the fire and smoke of battles! With you, I had secured a horseman's renown; why am I condemned to survive my glory and you?"

He bowed his head between his knees and was silent, while the khan bandaged his wound. Finally, noticing the care which the khan was bestowing on him, he suddenly exclaimed, —

"Leave me, Ackmeth Khan, leave an unhappy man to his hard fate. The journey is not over, and I yield. If you remain with me, you will needlessly perish with me. Look at that eagle circling above us; he knows that he will soon take my heart in his claws, and, thank God! it is better to be entombed in the breast of a noble bird than trampled underfoot by the Christians. Farewell! Leave me!"

[1] God be praised!

"Are you not ashamed, Ammalat, thus to succumb on stumbling against a straw? What is your wound? What's a dead horse? In eight days there will be no signs of your wound. We shall find a better horse. Misfortune comes from Allah, but so does good fortune. It is a sin to despair when one is young. Mount my horse, I will lead him by the bridle, and before nightfall we shall be at home. Come, every moment is precious; come, time is dear."

"Time no longer exists for me, Ackmeth Khan," answered the young man; "I thank you again for your fraternal friendship, but 1 will not abuse it. We have still too far to go, and we cannot walk so far. Leave me to my fate. On these heights, so near to heaven, I shall die free and content. My father is dead; I am wedded to a wife whom I do not love; my uncle and my father-in-law are on their knees to the Russians. Exiled from home, flying from battle, I ought not, nor do I wish, to live."

"Your fever is speaking, not you, Ammalat; your words are delirium. Are we not destined to survive our parents? As for your wife, our holy religion gives you the right to take three others. That you detest the chamkal, I can understand; but you ought to love his inheritance, which will some day make you a prince, and independent! Besides, a dead man has no need of wealth and power; a dead man takes no revenge, and it is for you to avenge yourself on the Russians. Rouse yourself, if only for that. We have been overcome; are we the first to experience reverses? To-day the Russians conquer; to-morrow it will be our turn. Allah grants happiness, but man wins his own renown. You are wounded and weak; but I am sound and strong. You are fainting with fatigue; while I am as fresh and active as a man who has not yet crossed the threshold of his room, who has just put on his sandals and girded his loins. Mount my horse, Ammalat, and, as sure as that eagle is not there to feast on your heart, — look! he is flying away and disappearing in the distance, — we will make the Russians pay dearly for our defeat of yesterday."

The face of Ammalat Beg brightened.

"Well, yes," he said, "you are right. I will live fc revenge, — for revenge, open or underhanded, but terrible, remorseless, deadly. Believe me, Ackmeth Khan, it is for the sake of revenge that I take up life again. From this moment I am yours, by the tomb of my father! I belong to you. Guide my steps, direct my blows, and, if ever I forget my oath, remind me of this moment, my dead horse, my bleeding hand, the eagle soaring above my head. If I fall asleep, I will waken and my poniard shall strike like the lightning."

Ackmeth Khan embraced the young man, took him in his arms like a child, and placed him in the saddle.

"And now," he said, "I recognize the pure blood of the emirs in you, — blood that riots in our veins like ignited saltpetre which, once fired, blasts mountains. Come with me, Ammalat Beg, and all that I have promised you Mahomet will make good."

And, while supporting the wounded man, Ackmeth Khan began to descend the mountain. Stones rolled from beneath their feet, more than once the horse fell, but at last, safe and sound, they reached the line where vegetation began.

Soon after, they entered a forest of many species of trees. The luxuriance of the forest and the oppressive stillness of the eternal twilight reigning under this green canopy impenetrable to the sun's rays, inspired man with respect for the savage freedom of nature.

At times the path threaded the forest trees, and again it was an escarpment on the edge of a cliff at whose foot glittered a brawling stream. Flame-throated pheasants sped from bush to bush. Everything exhaled that vivifying freshness of evening which is unknown to dwellers of the plain.

Our travellers had almost reached the village of Akhak, which is separated from Khunsack only by a small mountain, when they heard a shot.

They halted apprehensively.

But suddenly Ackmeth Khan announced, —

"They are my huntsmen; they are not expecting me at this hour, and especially in such a plight. I occasion Khunsack much joy and many tears."

Ackmeth Khan bowed his head and gave a sigh. His brow became clouded.

So quickly do sweet and bitter reflections succeed each other in an Asiatic's heart!

A second shot was heard, then a third. Then shot followed shot in quick succession.

"The Russians are at Khunsack!" cried Ammalat.

And he drew his sword, and dug his knees into his horse's sides, as if at a single leap he would clear the distance that intervened between him and them.

But the effort overpowered him; the sword slipped from his mutilated hand and fell to the earth.

As for him, he exerted his remaining strength to dismount from the horse.

"Ackmeth Khan," said he, "hasten to the aid of your people; your presence will avail more than the help of a hundred cavalrymen."

But Ackmeth Khan paid no attention; he was listening to the whistling balls as if he would distinguish those of the Russians from those of his own warriors.

SULTANETTA. 35

"How came they down there?" he cried. "Are they chamois-footed? have they eagles' wings? Farewell, Ammalat, I will go and die on the ruins of my own fortresses."

But just then a ball fell at his feet.

He picked it up, and, smiling, said composedly, —

"Remount my horse, Ammalat. You will soon know what that means; the Russian bullets are lead, and this is copper."

Then, looking at the ball, he said, —

"This blessed ally! it has come from where the Russians cannot, — from the south."

They proceeded to ascend the small hill that separated them from Khunsack.

Reaching the summit, they gazed down upon a veritable field of battle, beyond which rose the hamlet of Khunsack, overlooked by the two towers of the castle of Ackmeth Khan.

A hundred men, divided into two factions, were firing upon each other under cover of houses standing in front of great masses of rock or concealed behind them; while the women, unveiled, with babes in their arms and their hair flying, mingled with the combatants and urged them on.

Ammalat Beg regarded this spectacle with astonishment, and looked inquiringly at the Khan.

"That surprises you!" he said, shrugging his shoulders, "it is common with us. Down in the plain, when a man has a grudge against another man, he gives him a knife-thrust, and all is over; in the mountain, one man's quarrel is every man's quarrel. The reason of all that uproar? A trifle, very likely; perhaps a cow has been stolen. With us it is no disgrace to steal; the disgrace is to let oneself be robbed, that is all. Admire the courage of those women, Ammalat," pursued the khan excitedly, inhaling the powder-smoke with dilated nostrils. "The balls whiz past their ears; death flaps her wings above their heads, and they laugh at her. Oh, those are the mothers and wives of brave men, and truly it would be a pity were misfortune to overtake them! I am just in time to stop this game."

And, taking his gun, he advanced to the highest part of the ridge and discharged it into the air.

At that shot, coming from a direction whence it was not expected, the combatants faced about in amazement.

Then, with his left hand, Ackmeth Khan put back his bachlik.

There rose a great shout from both factions. The combatants had recognized him.

"Keep your powder and balls for the Russians, men of Khunsack," he cried; "not another shot. I will judge your difference, and give justice to him that is right and his deserts to him that is wrong."

But the khan's order was not needed for putting an end to the conflict; their joy at seeing him again was so great that all resentment seemed to be forgotten.

Men and women ran headlong toward him, crying, —

"Long live Ackmeth Khan!"

"That is well, that is well, my children!" responded Ackmeth Khan. "I will descend to-morrow to the public square and speak to the old men; but I bring back a wounded friend who is in need of prompt relief; do not hinder me then, for such relief he will find only at my house."

And, indeed, Ammalat Beg saw nothing of what was passing except as through a mist; he had abandoned the horse's bridle to maintain himself in the saddle.

In an instant they were shaping a litter from their

guns, all powder-blackened and hot from the fray. Friends and enemies joined together in spreading their bourkas across it. They laid the wounded man upon it; and Ackmeth Khan remounted his horse, as became a prince returning to his own stronghold.

Ammalat Beg was laid on the khan's softest rugs. He had fainted entirely away.

IV-

THE wounded man did not regain consciousness until the next day.

His ideas then returned to him like phantoms floating in mist.

He remembered nothing; he felt no pain.

This condition was agreeable rather than unpleasant. His torpor divested life of its sensibility and, consequently, of its bitterness.

He would have answered with equal indifference a summons to either life or death. He had neither the strength nor the desire to utter a word. Had his existence depended on a movement of the hand, he would not have taken the trouble to lift a finger.

This condition did not last long, however.

At noon, after the doctor's visit, when all the servants of the khan were at prayer, and he himself, according to his promise of the day before, had descended to the market-place, Ammalat Beg, left alone, thought he heard light and timid steps crossing the carpet of the room leading to his own.

With an effort he essayed to turn his head; and he must have succeeded in so doing, for he fancied he saw, — he was too weak to distinguish between fact and fancy, — he fancied, we repeat, that he saw the portière of his room lifted, and a young girl with black eyes, in a yellow silk robe confined by a red arkalouke decorated with buttons of enamel, with long black hair falling upon her shoulders, who very softly approached his bed, bending over him with sweet and tender solicitude to look at his wounded hand. Ammalat Beg, fanned by her breath, brushed by her raiment, felt a thrill of fire course his veins; then she poured the contents of a vial into a tiny silver cup, passed her arm under his head, raised it, and —

Ammalat felt nothing more, saw nothing more; his weighted eyelids sank again; all his senses seemed blended into a single one.

He listened.

He listened, and the rustling of the young girl's robe seemed to him the rustling of angel's wings.

But, this angel was flying away —

All became quiet again; and when the eyes of the wounded man reopened, he was alone, and it was impossible for him to invest his vision with any shadow of substance. Fragmentary trains of thought, floating like clouds in the immensity of space, were lost in feverish dreams; and as soon as he could utter a word, he said to himself, —

" It was a dream."

He was deceived.

What he believed to be a creation of delirium was a maid of sixteen, the daughter of Ackmeth Khan.

Among the mountaineers, even when Mussulmans, young girls enjoy infinitely greater freedom among men than do married women, although the Mohammedan law prescribes exactly to the contrary.

Now, Ackmeth Khan's daughter enjoyed even greater freedom than others, as it was only with her at his side that her father could rest from his fatigue; only with her did he unbend his brows in a smile. It meant salvation to the culprit if the young princess were but present when sentence was pronounced; the uplifted ax was arrested in air. To her everything was granted, for her everything was possible. Ackmeth Khan knew not how to deny her anything, and a suspicion had never entered his mind that the pure child could do anything incompatible with her duty or her rank. Besides, who could inspire her with the tender sentiments which might lead a young girl to commit a fault? Until now, her father had never received a guest who was his equal in birth; or rather, her heart had never concerned itself as to the rank or age of the guests who visited her father. That fact of itself had undoubtedly prolonged her girlhood, scarcely yet out of its childhood; but, since the evening before, she had been conscious of the beating of her own heart. On the day before, as she threw her arms about her father's neck, she had seen lying at his feet a young man in a swoon, almost dead. Her first feeling had been of fear, and she had turned her eyes away from the wounded man. But when her father had related why Ammalat came to be his guest, she began to view the young man with looks of melting pity; then, when the doctor had declared that his appalling weakness was due merely to loss of blood and not to the gravity of his wound, a tender anxiety possessed the young girl. Was the doctor not deceived? Such a gaping, ghastly wound — was it not more dangerous than he thought? She went to bed, full of this fear; all night in her dreams she saw the handsome youth covered with blood; more than once she opened her eyes in the dark, thinking she heard him moan; and, for the first time in her life, morning found her less fresh than the dawn; for the first time, she employed a ruse to gain a wish. Her father was in the wounded man's room; she chose this moment to bid her father good-morning. But Ammalat's eyes were closed, and she could not see his eyes. At noon she returned; Ammalat was alone, but the dazed eyes of the young prince closed at sight of her. The poor child was in despair. He must have such beautiful eyes! Never, in all her girlhood, had she so coveted a set of rich jewels. She would have given two diamonds the size of her own eyes to open those eyes that ought to beam with a fire very different, she thought, from that of two diamonds.

Finally, in the evening she returned again.

In the evening for the first time she encountered the invalid's wan but expressive clear eye; and, upon encountering it, the glance was not withdrawn. She knew very well what those eyes were crying to her: "Do not go away, star of my soul! Do you not perceive that you are my only light, and that, departing, you will plunge me into the darkness of night?"

She could not comprehend the change that was taking place in herself; it was impossible for her to tell whether she was still on earth or already in heaven. What she was experiencing, she had never experienced before: the blood surged to her heart so violently that she felt as if she were being smothered; it receded from her heart so quickly that she thought she was dying.

She had seen the eyes of the wounded man, and she had discovered that they were the most beautiful eyes in the world.

It remained for her to hear his voice.

But Ammalat Beg continued mute. Wholly absorbed in the contemplation of her, it did not occur to him to speak. What could be said that his eyes could not say as well as his voice?

The young girl's wishes were born in quick succession. With such fine eyes he must have a very sweet voice. What a pity not to hear that voice!

Then an idea occurred to her: if the young man did not speak, it was doubtless because he was too weak; if he were too weak to talk, certainly the wound was dangerous, more dangerous than the doctor had said.

Surely she could not go away filled with such dire uncertainty; and so she determined to speak first. What could be simpler? It was her duty to ask about his health.

A man would have to be a Tartar, would have to regard it as insulting to address a woman, must never have seen aught of one except a veil, and through this veil two eyebrows and perhaps the eyes beneath them, in order to conceive some idea of the thrill that sped through the veins of the wounded man, when, already pierced by her eyes, he received the girl's voice full in his heart.

And yet Sultanetta's words were very simple.

Her name was Sultanetta.

"How do you feel?" she asked.

"Oh! very well, very well," answered Ammalat Beg, trying to rise on his elbow; "so well that I am ready to die."

"Allah preserve you!" cried the girl, in dismay; "you must live yet a long time. Would you not be sorry to die?"

"To die in a happy hour is to die happy, Sultanetta; and were I to live a hundred years, I should never have a more fitting moment than this."

Sultanetta did not comprehend her guest's speech, but she understood the expression of his eyes, the accent of his voice. A flush tinged her cheek, and, with a sign warning the young man to lie back, she escaped from the room.

Among the mountaineers there are certainly skilful surgeons, especially those who treat wounds. They have secret remedies for closing wounds that are seemingly mysterious revelations of nature; but the most efficacious remedy acting on Ammalat Beg was the presence of the charming Sultanetta. At night he fell asleep with the fond hope that she would appear in his dream; in the morning he awoke to the certainty of seeing her in reality. His strength rapidly returned, and with his strength increased the feeling hitherto unknown which he had experienced at sight of Ackmeth Khan's daughter on that first day, and which was now so rooted in his heart as never again to leave it.

Ammalat Beg, as we have said, was married; but the marriage was arranged just as marriages in the Orient are arranged. Until the day of his wedding, he had never seen his betrothed; then, when he did see her, he found her ugly, and every sentiment akin to youth and love remained dormant in his heart. Following upon his marriage had come political wrangles with his uncle and his father-in-law. Tenderness, which among the Orientals appeals only to sensuality, was by degrees extinguished; so that his eyes on first beholding Sultanetta had no need to demand from his heart a sacrifice of the remains of an old love. The young man had been married, but his heart was virgin ground. Ardent by nature, independent from habit, Ammalat Beg abandoned himself completely to the sentiment by which he was possessed. To be with Sultanetta was his supreme happiness, and to look for her coming was his sole occupation when she was absent. He trembled on hearing her footsteps; he was shaken at the sound of her voice. Every tone filled his being with rapture. What he felt was like unto pain; but it was pain so sweet, an ill so full of recompense, that for want of this pain he doubted not he should die.

Doubtless these two young people, ignorant themselves of what they were experiencing, gave this unfamiliar sentiment the name of friendship; but, under no restraint, they were constantly together. Khan Ackmeth took frequent journeys in Avarie, and left his guest to his daughter. He only perhaps was aware of their love; but this love was the crown of his desires. A first marriage, as he had told Ammalat, was nothing to a Mussulman, who had the right to espouse four wives. Besides, he knew the scant affection existing between the young couple. To become the father-in-law of Ammalat Beg, that is, of the heir of Chamkal Tarkovsky, of a man who could be of such great assistance to him in his war with the Russians, was more than a desire, it was an ambition.

As for the two lovers, they made no calculations, we came near saying that they had no wishes. They were happy, asking nothing more, with no thought that this happiness could end. The days passed without their knowing how, in looking through the window at the mountains, at the flocks of sheep on the heights, at the rivers below. If Sultanetta was employed in embroidering her father's saddle, Ammalat was reclining near her on the cushions, telling her his youthful adventures, but oftener without speaking a word, his eyes being fixed upon hers. He thought not of the past, nor dreamed of the future. He only felt that he was happy, and, without removing the cup from his lips, he drank drop by drop the greatest felicity on earth for man, — to love and be loved.

Thus the summer went by.

One morning, one of the khan's shepherds came down in great fright.

At daybreak a tiger had come out of the forest, and,

creeping along like a cat towards the flock, had pounced on a sheep and carried it off.

The shepherd told it in the court, while all the noukars gathered around him in a circle.

"Well," said the khan, "does any one wish to kill the tiger? He may carry my finest and best gun. Let him kill the tiger, and the weapon is his."

One of the khan's noukars, an excellent shot, advanced, chose the weapon that pleased him best among all the khan's guns, and said,—

"I will go!"

The khan returned, related the incident to Sultanetta and Ammalat; but the young people were so engrossed by their love that neither of them appeared to hear what Ackmeth Khan had said.

The next day, they waited in vain for the noukar.

It was the shepherd's lad that came.

The boy told how, having arrived on the mountain towards evening, the noukar had discovered the tiger's path. The next morning before daylight he lay in ambush beside the trail that the animal had taken on leaving the forest to prowl for sheep.

But the tiger did not appear; yet he had been heard roaring in the forest about a verst away. Doubtless he had not devoured in one day the entire sheep, and had sufficient left for his morning meal.

Seeing that the tiger did not appear, the noukar had resolved to go in search of him. He had entered the forest. A quarter of an hour later, the boy had heard a report, then a roar; then all was silent.

He had waited an hour; but not seeing the man come out of the wood, he came to tell what had happened.

According to all probability, the man was dead.

They waited a day, two days, three days: the man had not been seen.

On the fourth day it was the tiger that put in an appearance, and he carried off a second sheep.

The little herder ran in terror to announce the ferocious brute's second attack.

This time it chanced that Sultanetta was sprinkling the flowers in her window, when the herder entered the court.

She heard all that the boy was saying.

She went back to Ammalat Beg and told him what she had just learned.

Ammalat Beg had not listened to a word of what Ackmeth Khan had said, but Sultanetta's words were too precious for a single one to be lost.

Ackmeth Khan entered just as Sultanetta was finishing her story.

"Well," he demanded, "what do you say to that, Ammalat?"

"That I have always desired to go on a tiger-hunt," returned the young man, "and that I am grateful to Allah for fulfilling my desire. I will try my luck against the tiger."

Sultanetta looked at Ammalat, pale but smiling; she understood, and, although filled with apprehension, she was proud.

Ackmeth Khan shook his head.

"A tiger is not the boar of Daghestan, Ammalat."

"Put me on the tiger's trail, and I will follow it as though it were a wild boar's."

"Tiger's tracks often lead to death," insisted Ackmeth Khan, who, having begun to be alarmed at his young friend's listlessness, with delight saw him emerge from his lethargy.

"Do you think my head will whirl on a slippery path, and that I cannot go where your noukar has been? If the heart of an Avare is as stout as mountain granite, the heart of a native of Daghestan is as hard as her steel."

Smiling, Ackmeth Khan extended a hand to him.

"And your heart's steel, brother, will break the tiger's teeth and the eagle's hooked beak. And when will you start?"

"Two hours before dawn."

"Very well," said Ackmeth Khan; "I will find you a guide."

"He is already found," said a voice behind the two men.

Ackmeth Khan, turning, recognized Nephtali.

"Ah! it is you?" he said.

"Yes, I heard that a tiger had eaten one of your sheep and killed a noukar, and I have come to say, My father's friend, I wish to prove that I am good for something else than waylaying travellers on the mountains to offer hospitality. I have come to slay the tiger."

"That may be," said Ammalat; "but you come too late."

"Why so?" said the young Tchetchen. "We shall be two on the trail and two in the fight. My father's son is entitled to walk beside a prince, were the prince Chamkal Tarkovsky's nephew. Ask Ackmeth Khan."

"I need no help to accomplish my undertaking," said the young man haughtily.

"There is no doubt that you need no one," said Ackmeth; "but you are wrong to refuse the companion who offers of his own free will to share your danger. I advise you to accept Nephtali's offer. Exchange vows like two brave abrecks, and may Allah watch over you!"

Ammalat's eyes turned toward Sultanetta. The young girl was regarding him with clasped hands. She knew

Nephtali to be one of the boldest and most skilful hunters in the mountain, and she would not be sorry that Ammalat should be accompanied by one of whose courage she was sure.

"So be it!" said Ammalat.

And he extended his hand to the youth.

Among the Avares and Tchetchens, when two men are engaging in a common danger together, it is their custom to swear on the Koran not to abandon each other.

If one of the two fails to keep his oath, he is thrown over a precipice with his back to the abyss, as becomes a coward and a traitor.

The two young men descended to the mosque, and took the oath of abrecks. The mullah blessed their weapons, and they set out upon the mountain road amidst the cheers of the crowd.

"Both, or neither!" cried the khan after them.

"We will bring back the tiger's skin, or die," returned the hunters.

Ammalat did not say good-bye to Sultanetta; but, on the highest tower of the khan's palace, the young girl stood waving her handkerchief.

And the handkerchief fluttered until the two young men had disappeared in the mountain.

It is unnecessary to observe that Ammalat Beg walked behind, and was the last to lose sight of the village.

V.

THE next day passed.

They did not hope to have much news of the hunters for the first twenty-four hours.

Then came the following day, and the night.

On that evening the old men were worn out with gazing down the road.

They had seen nothing.

There was perhaps not a fireside in all Khunsack at which the expedition of the two abrecks was not being discussed; but of all hearts, the saddest and most anxious was Sultanetta's.

If a shout was heard in the court, if a step echoed from the stairway, her blood bounded madly through her veins, she was unable to breathe, she ran to the window, she inquired at the gate, and, deceived for the twentieth time, with bowed head and misty eyes she would resume her work, which for the first time seemed shockingly tedious. All her questions, without her tongue's framing Ammalat's name, had reference to Ammalat. She asked her father and brothers what kind of wounds the tiger inflicted, at what distance he could be seen, how long it would take him to reach the village from the place where he had been seen ; and after every question she would droop her head sadly and say to herself, —

"They are lost!"

The third day proved that they had not felt uneasiness without cause.

About two o'clock in the afternoon, a pale young man, his clothes torn, covered with clots of blood, and exhausted by hunger and fatigue, arrived at the outskirts of the village.

It was Nephtali. They pressed around him with curiosity, and eagerly questioned him.

This is what he had to tell: —

"On the same day that we left Khunsack, we discovered traces of the beast; but it was late, darkness was coming on; we might lose his trail, wander away, and expose ourselves to him without defence. We would reserve the attack for the morrow.

"I knew of a cave a hundred steps away; we entered that. A rock blocked up the entrance, and we slept tranquilly on our bourkas.

"The next morning at daybreak, we awoke; a roar that we heard in the mountain, told us that it was time to bestir ourselves.

"We examined the priming of our guns; we cleaned the barrels with our ramrods, assured ourselves that our kandjiars played freely in their sheaths, and set off.

"The farther we went in the forest, the narrower the path became, and the more significant were the traces of the tiger.

"Flecks of blood, broken bones, and shreds of flesh said plainly, 'This is the tiger's path.'

"On the way we found intact the two hands of a man: they were undoubtedly those of Ackmeth Khan's noukar.

"It is known that man-eating beasts which devour the entire body dare not touch the hands, which typify man's rule over nature.

"We advanced cautiously, step by step; evidently we were nearing the tiger's lair.

SULTANETTA.

"Suddenly we came upon a glade white with bones. In the midst lay the tiger, and, having feasted, he was tossing a head, like a young kitten playing with a wooden ball.

"An ambitious desire took possession of me for which I deserve blame: it was to kill the tiger alone, without concerning myself about my companion. I took aim at the tiger and fired.

"Where did I hit him? I cannot tell. But through the smoke, before it could clear, I saw a tawny streak flash through the air, and at the same moment I felt as if Mount Elburz[1] were descending upon my head.

"I saw nothing more, heard nothing more, unless it were a cry and a shot.

"I had fainted.

"How long I was unconscious I do not know. When I again opened my eyes, it seemed, from the freshness in the air and the position of the sun, that the sun had been up for an hour or two.

"All around was quiet.

"I still had my gun in my hand.

"Ammalat's gun, broken into two pieces, was ten paces to the right of the spot where I had fallen.

"The stones were covered with blood; but whose blood? Ammalat's, or the tiger's?

"The bushes all about were torn up by their roots.

"It was evident that a terrible, maddening, deadly struggle had taken place.

"And yet I could find the body of neither man nor animal.

"I called Ammalat with all my strength, but no one answered.

"I wished to follow the tiger's trail, to find Ammalat

[1] One of the highest three of the mountains of the Caucasus.

alive, or to die on his body; but I was so weak that at the end of a hundred steps I was forced to sit down.

"Suddenly a hope sprang up: perhaps he had killed the tiger, and, believing me dead, had returned to Khunsack.

"I mustered all my strength again and took the road back to the village. You have not seen him?

"Brothers, I come like a crushed serpent; my head is in your hands. I have abandoned my kounack in danger; do with me as you see fit.

"Whatever your verdict, I will not complain. If you think I have deserved death, I will die resignedly.

"If you leave me my life, I will live blessing you.

"Allah is my witness that I have done all that a man could do — "

A murmur rose among the listeners.

Some excused Nephtali; others blamed him; all pitied him.

The popular opinion was that Nephtali had fled, abandoning Ammalat; that he had invented the whole story that he had just related; that, in short, he had betrayed his kounack.

His wounds were but slight; how could the tiger's blow have produced such a long, deep fainting-spell?

Then other suspicions began to creep out.

Nephtali had been almost raised in the house of Khan Ackmeth, who was, as we know, his father's kounack.

He had ceased coming to the village, they said, because he was in love with the beautiful Sultanetta, and was not of high enough birth, although all mountaineers are equal, to wed the khan's daughter.

In the village there were rumors of a probable union between Ammalat and Sultanetta.

Instigated by jealousy, might not Nephtali have left Ammalat to die, or even have killed him?

When a wicked thought enters the head, it is like bad seed let fall on good ground; it sprouts more quickly and more vigorously than the other, takes up all the room, crowds out the other, and at last is alone.

But one cry rose above all others, one conviction prevailed over all the rest.

"Take him to Ackmeth Khan; Ackmeth Khan shall decide."

And with a great uproar the crowd directed itself towards the castle.

Sultanetta heard the clamor, she ran to the window, she saw the crowd: amid the crowd she searched for Ammalat Beg.

Then she recognized Nephtali, — Nephtali alone!

She too, poor child, who had never thought ill of her neighbor, was inspired by a wicked thought.

She ran to the flight of steps just as her father also arrived and Nephtali, conducted by the people, was entering the court.

He bowed before the khan.

"Speak," said Ackmeth.

Nephtali told the same story without altering a word of it.

Sultanetta listened, rigid, cold, motionless, silent as a statue.

"Coward!" Ackmeth Khan contented himself with saying. "By good luck, you are not an Avare, but a Tchetchen."

"By the bones of my father, whose death you announced, I have told the truth," answered Nephtali; "now dispose of me as you will."

"You took your oath," said Ackmeth Khan, "to return with your comrade or with the tiger's skin. You vowed to die, if you failed to keep your oath. You have not kept it, you must die."

"When?" asked Nephtali.

"I give you three days, during which a search shall be made. If in those three days Ammalat is not found, or some proof of your innocence is not forthcoming, you shall die. — Hear, all of you," said Ackmeth Khan to the crowd, "I grant him three days. During those three days let no one rail at him, let no one insult him, let no one touch a single hair of his head; but if he tries to escape, you may shoot him as you would a dog. — Son of Mohammed Ali, I have judged you as your father would have judged you."

And to his noukars, —

"Take him away," he added; "you shall answer for him with your heads."

Then, bringing his papak down over his eyes, he said to Sultanetta, —

"Come, let us go in. If we do not discover Ammalat alive, he shall at least be avenged."

Nephtali was conducted to the prison within the fortress.

That same day, thirty mountaineers set out armed as for battle; they were going in search of Ammalat Beg.

It was a point of honor with Ackmeth Khan, if he did not find Ammalat alive, to secure at least his bones and give them burial.

Often do the Avares rush into the hottest of the affray to rescue from the Russian's hands their slain friend or chief, and then fall upon his corpse, preferring to die with him rather than to abandon him.

Sultanetta had quitted her father's arm, and returned to her own room. In appearance she seemed calm; she did not complain, she did not weep.

Yet her mother spoke to her and she did not answer. The sparks from her father's chibouk burnt holes in her dress, but she gave no heed. The wind blew down from the mountain, and to it she exposed her bared head.

The most antagonistic sentiments were struggling in her heart and breaking it. But the heart was far from the eyes : not a muscle in her face betrayed its suffering.

The pride of the daughter of the khan was struggling with Sultanetta's love, and it would have been impossible to tell whether pride or love would yield.

Thus she passed the remainder of the day.

At night, left alone, she was able to weep at her ease.

She opened the window, leaned her elbow upon it, and kept her eyes fixed on the mountain.

It seemed to her as if at every instant she should hear some sound announcing Ammalat's return, — her own name issuing from the night in his dear voice, a song of joy or a cry of pain.

She heard only the plaintive wailing of jackals, those slaves of the tiger and lion, whom these sultans of mountain and desert use for toling their prey, and the distant, ceaseless roar of the cascade which falls from the summit of Gaudour d'Ach.

This sound recalled a walk that she had often taken with Ammalat Beg.

It led to the ruins of a Christian monastery — the Avares became Mohammedans less than two centuries ago — situated two versts to the west of Khunsack. The hand of time had respected the church, and man, strange to say, had wrought no greater destruction than time. It had remained intact, surrounded by the débris of other structures; but the ivy had crept in at the broken windows and spread its mantle of sober green over the interior; the trees had pushed through crevices between the stones, making the gaps wider and wider; a moss as fine as the finest carpet spread itself over the flags, its freshness being maintained by a spring which had made an opening through the wall, and which ran clear as liquid crystal down the whole length of the chapel, making it a delicious retreat on hot summer days.

Often had Sultanetta come with Ammalat, together with Sakina, her attendant, to sit under the cool dome and dream to the murmur of the brooklet; then, sometimes, a mountain goat, coming to slake his thirst, frightened at the sight of the two young people, would bound away in flight.

"To-morrow," said she, "I will go without you to the chapel, where so often I have gone with you, dear Ammalat Beg."

And, tired of the jackals' wailing, which seemed to her a bad omen, the young girl closed the window again and cast herself upon her bed.

In the morning she called Sakina, and said, —

"We will take a walk along the banks of the Urens."

On the way, Sultanetta thought with sweet sadness of that charming spot, so lovely, so fresh, so peaceful.

It seemed to her, on reaching the convent, that it would be a profanation not to enter alone with her remembrances.

She sent Sakina to gather some wild mulberries, telling her to return and look for her near the stream; then she crossed the mossy threshold of the chapel.

The dim light of the church, the twittering of the swallows which had nested there in the spring, the murmuring stream, all combined to dissolve in tears the grief that oppressed her heart.

She sat down at the water's brink, and as through a mist watched her tears falling into the water.

Suddenly she heard the sound of a step too firm to be Sakina's. She lifted her head and shrieked with terror.

Before her stood a man covered with dirt and blood. A tiger's skin, the head of which enframed his face, fell from his shoulders to the ground.

Sultanetta's first cry had been a shriek of terror; the second was a cry of joy.

Through all the dust, mire, and blood by which he was stained, beneath the tiger's skin she recognized Ammalat Beg.

Then, forgetting everything else in the world, she sprang to her feet, and with a bound, filled with joy and love, she cast herself into his arms.

A cry escaped Ammalat also; his mouth, like a bee, lit upon the rosy lips of the young girl. They had no need of words.

This time, quite beside himself, the young man exclaimed,—

" And you love me then, Sultanetta?"

Abashed at her own boldness, blushing red under her lover's kiss, the girl withdrew her lips from Ammalat's, and gently repelled him.

Overcome with terror, and ready to let her slip from his arms, Ammalat Beg demanded,—

"Then you do not love me?"

"Allah save me!" said the innocent girl, drooping the eyelids, but not the eyes. "Love! what terrible word have you spoken?"

"It is the sweetest word in all the universe, Sultanetta! The sun is love! the Spring is love! the flowers are love!"

"Ammalat," said the young girl, "a year ago, a woman uttering frightful shrieks rushed out from her house without a veil, and, all bleeding, fell in the dust at my feet. A man was pursuing her with a poniard in his hand. I fled to the castle: but it seemed to me that the woman was following me. For a long time after, I would waken at night thinking that I heard her shrieks, and in the darkness I could see her again all bleeding and grovelling on the earth. When I asked why this unhappy woman had been killed, and what had been her crime that her murderer was not punished, they answered, 'She loved a young man.'"

"Oh! it was not because she loved him that she was killed, dear child."

"Why was it, then?"

"It was because she had betrayed the one she loved."

"Betrayed! what does that mean? I do not understand, Ammalat."

"Please God you may never understand!"

Then, mustering his heart's whole tenderness into his voice, —

"You love me, do you not, Sultanetta?"

"I think so," said the young girl.

"Well, do you think that you would ever feel for another what you feel for me?"

"Never!" cried Sultanetta, quickly.

"That, you see, would be betraying me — "

Sultanetta turned upon Ammalat the eyes of an Oriental woman, to which the poets find only the eye of the gazelle to compare.

"Oh!" exclaimed she, "if you but knew, Ammalat, what I have suffered during the four days in which I have not seen you! I did not know what absence meant. When my brothers or my father go away, I weep at saying good-bye. True, I said good-bye to you without weeping; but I have wept enough since, I am sure! Listen, Ammalat," continued the girl; "I have discovered one thing that I will tell you: I could not live without you."

"And I," said the young man, "not only cannot live without you, but I am ready to die for you, my darling, to sacrifice not only my life but my soul for you."

There was a sound of footsteps: Sakina was returning with her hands filled with wild mulberries.

She uttered a cry of fright at seeing the young man; but on recognizing him she exclaimed,—

"Oh, prince, then you are not dead?"

These words reminded Sultanetta that she was not the only one anxious about Ammalat, but that her father was impatiently awaiting news, and that there was a poor prisoner whose life depended on Ammalat's return.

On the way, the young beg gave Sultanetta an account of what had happened between himself and the tiger.

Of the first part of the adventure, Nephtali had told the exact truth.

This is what followed: —

Just as Nephtali had fallen under the tiger, Ammalat Beg fired a shot.

The ball from Ammalat's gun broke the creature's lower jaw.

At the same instant the tiger abandoned Nephtali and sprang upon Ammalat, who awaited him, pistol in hand, and then, dodging lightly to one side, fired close to his muzzle.

The bullet penetrated eye and brain.

Overpowered with pain, the animal began to leap in the air and roll on the earth. He acted as if blind and mad.

Ammalat threw down his pistol, took his gun by the barrel, approached the tiger, and dealt him a terrible blow on the head.

The gun flew into fragments.

The animal seemed to acknowledge himself to be vanquished, and tried to run. One of his fore paws had been shattered by Nephtali, one jaw was hanging, and an eye was missing from its socket.

But, mutilated as he was, he made swifter progress than Ammalat Beg.

Ammalat Beg set out to follow him, while reloading his pistol. From time to time he found places where the animal had stopped and struggled in torment. In such places the blood-saturated earth was pawed, the grass was plucked up, the bushes were in splinters.

From time to time he caught sight of the animal dragging himself along with difficulty, crawling rather than walking. Then he would hasten his own pace; but, as soon as the tiger felt himself to be pursued, he increased his own efforts and gained on the hunter.

This sort of chase lasted all day without rest or relaxation.

Night fell; Ammalat Beg was forced to stay during the night, or he might have lost the animal's trail.

He had abandoned his bourka, his papak and tchouka, everything that could impede his course: for clothing, he had nothing left but his bechmet and trousers; for arms, only his kandjiar and pistol.

In the morning he awoke chilled and famished.

As soon as the light would admit, he again took up the tiger's trail.

It was not long before he found him.

But, this time, despairing of escape by flight, the tiger not only awaited him, but he even came creeping towards him.

The ferocious brute could no longer stand, he could not raise himself; his strength was exhausted from loss of blood.

Ammalat Beg met him half-way. He halted at ten paces from him.

SULTANETTA.

One of the tiger's eyes was put out, but the other glowed like a live coal. Ammalat Beg, whose pistol never missed a rouble in air, placed a bullet in the other eye as deftly as with his hand.

The animal leaped into the air, fell over on his back, stretched out his three frightful paws in his last agony, — the fourth being broken, — stiffened, yielded up his breath in one roar, and was dead.

Ammalat Beg flung himself upon him; it was the famished man, this time, who seemed ready to devour the tiger.

With his poniard he opened an artery in the neck, and sucked the blood that flowed from it.

He then laid open the breast and ate a piece of the heart yet warm. — The Arabs of Algeria on killing a lion make their sons eat the still bleeding heart to render them brave; the Greeks in like manner eat the hearts of eagles. — He next skinned the animal with his kandjiar, and threw the hide over his shoulders.

Not until then did he look about him; it was a drizzly morning, a dense fog began to spread over the mountain; he was unable to distinguish objects ten paces away.

He crouched down upon a rock and waited.

The day went by, and night came on; he heard the whirring of the eagles as they regained their eyries amid the clouds.

He built a fire with powder and dry leaves, by the aid of his pistol.

A bit of the tiger's heart broiled over the coals furnished his supper.

Then, spreading the animal's skin with the fur uppermost, he rolled up in it and went to sleep.

He was awakened in the morning by the first rays of

the sun; knowing that Khunsack lay to the east, he proceeded eastward.

Arriving at the outskirts of the wood, he beheld Khunsack bleaching on the rocks.

He was thirsty: the tiger had no more blood with which to quench his thirst. Ammalat Beg recalled the pure rill which ran through the chapel.

He descended by the shortest route, over rocks and cliffs, holding on by tufts of grass, the roots of trees, or jutting stones.

He at length reached the valley.

He ran to the chapel with the speed of a thirsting deer.

But on entering, he saw a woman, heard a cry, recognized Sultanetta.

He forgot everything, — hunger, thirst, fatigue; everything but his love.

" Glory to God, and thanks! "

As Ammalat Beg pronounced these, the last words of his story, he, together with the young maiden and her attendant, reached the outskirts of Khunsack.

The shout sent up by those who perceived them ran the whole length of the hamlet with the swiftness of a train of gunpowder.

Every dweller in Khunsack rushed out of his house, forming a procession after the two young people.

The cry of " Ammalat Beg! Ammalat Beg! " startled Ackmeth Khan in the depths of his harem.

He reached the head of the flight of steps in front of the castle just as the two young people had attained its foot.

In spite of the efforts that he made to remain grave and sedate, as every good Mussulman should in the face of grief or joy, he held out his arms to Ammalat Beg.

As if there were something for which she ought to be pardoned, Sultanetta sprang forward simultaneously with her lover to her father's breast, and he enveloped them both in the same embrace, welcomed them both with the same kiss.

"Dear father," said Sultanetta, "we have been unjust to Nephtali; everything happened as he said."

The khan gave an order for the prisoner to be released.

Then he had an ox and six sheep killed, in order that Ammalat's return might be an occasion of feasting throughout the entire village.

But when Ammalat had told Ackmeth Khan what he had already told Sultanetta, he sent for Nephtali.

"Nephtali," said he, "all justice is done you. If you will enter my household, you shall be made chief of my noukars."

"I thank you, Ackmeth Khan," was the young man's reply; "I am a Tchetchen, and not an Avare. I came to kill the tiger that was preying on your sheep; the tiger is dead, I have no more to do here. Farewell, Ackmeth Khan."

He approached Ammalat Beg, and held out his hand.

"Farewell, kounack; for life, for death!" said he.

Then, passing Sultanetta, he bowed low and said, —

"Shine forever, O morning star!"

And he departed with the gait of a king leaving the throne-room.

Ackmeth Khan waited until the door was again closed.

"And now, Ammalat Beg," said he, "be doubly welcome. After the tiger-hunt, that of the lion. To-morrow we march against the Russians."

"Allah!" exclaimed Sultanetta sadly; "more expeditions! more deaths! When will blood cease to flow on the mountain?"

"When the mountain streams shall descend into the valley as milk, when sugar-cane shall grow at the summit of Elburz," rejoined Ackmeth Khan with a smile.

VI.

How grand is the Terek as it thunders through the Pass of Dariel! There, like a genie deriving his power from Heaven, he struggles with nature. In some places he flashes between rocky precipices glittering like a drawn sword which is piercing the granite wall; in others, dull and foaming, he struggles with enormous boulders along his course, overturning them as he goes and carrying them with him. On dark nights, when the belated horseman passes along the steep bank which controls it, he draws his bourka close about him. Not all the horrors to be conjured up by the most fantastic imagination can compare with the reality by which he is surrounded. The flood, swollen by the rains, rolls underneath his feet with a booming sound, and plunges from ledges of rock above his head, threatening each moment to crush him. A sudden flash rends the obscurity, and the terrified traveller sees only the gloomy cloud above him, and below him a hideous chasm. Everywhere are precipitous walls, before, behind, beside him; and, leaping from ledge to ledge, the maddened Terek is dashed into lustrous foam. For the moment, its swift waters, as troubled as the spirits of hell, writhe at the foot of a precipice with terrible din, and seem in the abyss like a throng of spectres driven by an archangel's sword. Great boulders follow the current of the stream with ominous crashing, and then it is that, blinded anew by a flying serpent of fire, he suddenly finds himself plunged into a sea of darkness; then, in turn, the thunder rumbles, the rocks vibrate with a sound as of a cascade of mountains rolling over and over each other. Earth's echo is answering heaven's artillery, and again the flash, and again night, then the thunderbolt, then once again the sound of tumbling mountains. And, as if the whole chain of the Caucasus, from Taman to Apsheron, were shaking its granite shoulders, a shower of rattling stones comes hurtling down, striking with a rebound. Your horse stops dismayed, backs away, falls on his haunches, rears. His mane, whipped by the wind, lashes your face; a spirit moans in the air, as doleful as a lost soul. A shiver passes through you, and perspiration stands in beads on your face; your heart shrinks, and in spite of you there rises to your lips the prayer that your mother taught you when you were a child.

And yet, what charm, what softness the rosy-browed, fair-footed Morning brings to the gorge where the Terek roars! The clouds, chased by the wind, rise from the earth and hover about the icy peaks; above them a glow of light throws up the silhouette of the eastern mountains; the rocks glisten, silvered over with raindrops; and the Terek, still dark, still raging, still foaming, bounds over the stones as if seeking a broad bed in which to rest.

However, one thing is wanting in the Caucasus,— rivers and lakes in which these giants of creation can mirror themselves. The Terek, writhing in the depths of gorges, looks like a stream, a torrent at the most; but, below Vladikafkas, upon entering the valley, it spreads the stones brought with it from the mountains and flows broadly and at will, still swift but less boisterous, as if resting and regaining breath, exhausted after its painful toil. At last, having cleared the head of the Little

SULTANETTA. 67

Kabardah, it turns eastward, like a pious Mussulman, and, overflowing both banks, always at war with each other, it hastens across the steppes past Kisliar to cast itself into the Caspian Sea.

But, before reaching its long resting-place, it has already paid its tribute, and, like a rugged workman, has turned the great wheels of the mills. Along its right bank between the woods and the mountains, are scattered the Aoubs and Kabardians, whom we confound by giving them the general name of Circassians, with the Tchetchens below them and nearer the sea. These Aoubs are conquered, but only on the outside; in reality they are bands of outlaws, who derive profit from both their friendliness with the Russians and their proceeds from mountain brigandage; having free access to all places, they forewarn their countrymen of the movements of the soldiers, of the numbers of their garrisons, of the state of their fortresses; they conceal them in their dwellings when on an expedition, share with them, or buy, the booty when they return, furnish them salt and Russian powder, and often assist in person on their expeditions. The worst of it is that hostile mountaineers, wearing the same costume as those who have submitted, pass the Terek without hindrance, approach travellers without being recognized, attack them if they are the stronger, and if the weaker, pass them with a bow, the hand on the heart.

It is the way of the vanquished.

And, as regards these last, we must say, their position opposite to their terrible neighbors drives them almost involuntarily into this duplicity. Knowing that, hindered by the obstacle which the river presents to them, the Russians would not have time to come to their defence against the mountaineers, they are forced to take their compa triots by the hand; but at the same time they pretend to be friendly with the Russians, before whom they quail. Every one of them in the morning is ready to become the kounack of a Russian, and, in the evening, the guide of a mountaineer.

As to the left bank of the Terek, it is covered with rich stanitzas belonging to the Cossacks on the border. Between these stanitzas lie rude villages. The Cossacks, moreover, differ in no way from the mountaineers except in their unshaven heads; but, aside from that, their weapons, clothes, and ways are the same. It is a fine thing to watch them in a bout with mountaineers. It is not, properly speaking, a fight, but a tournament in which each strives to show off superiority of strength and courage. Two Cossacks will charge bravely on four horsemen, and, with equal numbers, they will always come off conquerors. All speak Tartar, all know the mountaineers. Sometimes they are relatives, even, by reason of the women whom they have kidnapped; but in the field they are mortal enemies. Although the Cossacks are strictly forbidden to cross the Terek, yet the bravest of them swim across, sometimes on pleasure, sometimes on business. For their part, when night comes, the mountaineers do the same; they crouch in the grass, creep through the bushes, and suddenly stand up in the traveller's path, taking him prisoner and setting a ransom on his head if he makes no resistance, but killing him if he does.

It even happens that the most enterprising spend two or three days in the vineyards near the village awaiting an opportunity to do a stroke of business. That is why the border Cossack never leaves his house unarmed, never takes a step without his trusty poniard, nor goes into the field without his gun. He ploughs, sows, cultivates, and mows his piece of ground, always armed. That is why the mountaineers avoid the stanitzas and usually prey upon the rude villages, or boldly strike into the interior of the provinces.

In this case a fight is inevitable, and the most daring horsemen eagerly engage in it for the sake of fame, which they value above everything, even above booty.

During the autumn of 1819, when the events we are relating occurred, Kabardians and Tchetchens, taking advantage of the absence of General Scrinokof, had mustered fifteen hundred men to plunder certain villages lying on the other side of the Terek, to take prisoners and carry off flocks.

Their chief was the Kabardian prince, Djemboulat.

Ammalat Beg, coming to him with a letter from Ackmeth Khan, had been very well received, and he would have been made chief of a division, had there been any such position or any regular troops among these bands. His horse and his individual courage assign to each man his place in the combat. At first, there is some question as to how to begin the affair, and how to engage the enemy; but eventually there is neither command nor obedience, and the fight is conducted at random to the end.

After warning the neighboring princes who were to take part in the expedition with him, Djemboulat appointed a place of meeting, and, at a given signal, was heard through all the hamlets the cry, " *Guaray! guaray!* " that is, " To arms! to arms! " and in a few hours Kabardian and Tchetchen riders were coming from all directions.

Fearing treachery, no one except the chief knew where the night would be spent, or where the river would be crossed. Dividing themselves into small bands, the mountaineers gained the subjugated hamlets and waited there for night. The vanquished received their compatriots with every kind of joyful demonstration; but the distrustful Djemboulat was not carried away by this apparent loyalty. He placed sentinels on all sides, proclaiming to the inhabitants that whoever under any pretext tried to cross over the border would be run through without mercy. Most of the horsemen lodged in the houses of their relatives and friends; but Djemboulat and Ammalat Beg camped in the field, lying before the fire, as long as was necessary to rest their horses.

Djemboulat's mind was occupied with the Russians and the fight in which he was about to engage; but Ammalat Beg was far from the battle-field; his thoughts took eagle's wings, and flew beyond the mountains of Avarie; and his heart, forced to remain far from the one it loved, was full of sorrow. The sound of the mountain *balalaïka*, accompanied by a monotonous chant, diverted his sadness; he listened in spite of himself.

A Kabardian was singing this old song, —

> "Toward snowy Kasbek's towering peak,
> Far from the wheat, far from the rye,
> As eagle birds their eyries seek,
> The stormy clouds go wheeling by.

> "Who are these speeding cavaliers
> Through fog and mist and white with frost ?
> Ah! Allah, save! — our mountaineers,
> Our heroes flee, the battle's lost.

> "The Russian hordes are at their heels,
> Mount higher, braves, and faster, braves,
> The craggy steeps! The laggard feels
> Death's cohorts press with naked glaives.

SULTANETTA.   71

"High up, and higher, Kasbek grows
A wooded slope whose leafage clads
A refuge from the foeman's blows.
Ha! higher! faster! courage, lads!

"False fate yields valor to the foe:
Their chargers pant, they toil in vain,
And naught can save, — oh, woe! oh, woe!
That mount should vanquished be by plain.

"But, hark! a pious mullah's prayer
From bended knees, — *Death, listening, hears,* —
Goes speeding through the lambent air,
And reaches Allah's heeding ears.

"To save his faithful, Allah bids
The wood obey Mahomet's call;
That fortress sure all danger rids.
To prophet praise! God's over all!"

"Yes, in other times it was so," said Djemboulat, with a smile. "Our fathers believed in prayer, and God heard them; but now, my friend, the finest refuge is courage, the surest prayer, a schaska. Take heed, Ammalat," he continued, caressing his mustache. "I do not hide from you the fact that it will be a warm encounter. The colonel has mustered his command. But where is he? How many men has he? That is something that I do not know, something that none of us know."

"So much the better!" said Ammalat, composedly; "the more Russians the better the mark."

"Yes, but the more difficulty there will be in getting away with the booty."

"Little the booty matters to me. I wish vengeance and seek glory."

"Glory is well when it lays golden eggs, Ammalat.

It is a disgrace to show empty hands to one's wife. Winter is approaching; in order to regale one's friends, one must lay in his provisions at the expense of the Russians. Choose your position beforehand, Ammalat: march in the vanguard, or remain near me with the abrecks."

"I go where there is danger; but what is the oath among these abrecks?"

"Each has his own: here is one of the bravest. They vow to expose themselves for a longer or shorter period to every kind of peril, to grant no grace to enemies, to pardon no offender, not even a friend, not even a brother; to take whatever pleases them, especially when the thing that pleases presents itself to view. This oath taken, the man who has taken it can kill, pillage, plunder, without being punished. He is fulfilling a vow. Abrecks of this sort are bad friends, but good enemies."

"And," inquired Ammalat Beg, a dweller of the plain to whom the customs of the mountaineer were for the most part unknown, "what induces these horsemen to take such oaths?"

"Some take them from excessive courage, others from excessive poverty, others again because they are a prey to some sorrow. There, for instance, — notice that Kabardian rubbing up his gun rusted by the night-fog; well, he became an abreck for five years because his mistress died of small-pox. During those five years you might better have a tiger for a friend than him for a comrade. He has already been wounded three times, and every wound, instead of curbing, spurs him on."

"Singular custom! And how does an abreck return to his family after such a life?"

"Quite naturally; the past is past. The abreck forgets it, and the neighbors are wary of remembering it.

Freed from his oath, he becomes as gentle as a lamb. But it is quite dark; the Terek is shrouded in fog: it is time."

Djemboulat gave a whistle, and his whistle was instantly carried along the entire line of the camp. In less than five minutes all were in the saddle. After deciding upon the best place to cross the Terek, the little company descended quietly to the river bank. Ammalat Beg admired the stillness, not merely of the soldiers, but also of the horses. Not one whinnied on the way. Each in placing his feet seemed fearful of causing the stones to roll and of thus warning the enemy. They soon reached the river's edge. The water was low; a headland, half sand, half stones, jutted out towards the opposite bank. The whole company, by employing double the time, could have crossed at that point almost dry-footed; but half of the troops ascended the river to swim across and hide the principal passage from the Cossacks. Those who were sure of their horses leaped straight from the bank into the stream. Others tied leathern bottles to their horses; the swift current bore them away, but they finally reached the bank and scaled it wherever they were able. A dense fog had spread, apparently to conceal all their movements.

It is essential for the reader to know that all along the Terek — on the left bank of the river — there exists a line called the border watch. Cossacks were stationed on every hillock. As you pass during the day, you notice on each rise of ground a tall post with a cask at its extremity. This cask is full of straw, and ready to light at the first cry of alarm. To this pole a saddled horse is constantly tied, and near it, lying on the ground, is the sentinel.

At night the watch is doubled.

But, in spite of all these precautions, the mountaineers, wrapped in their bourkas, enveloped in darkness and surrounded by fog, pass between the pickets like water through a sieve.

This time, also, it happened thus. The subjugated mountaineers, knowing the Cossack picket-posts marvellously well, were placed at the head of each band, and conducted it through the line.

At only a single point was there bloodshed.

Djemboulat himself struck the blow.

On reaching the opposite bank of the Terek, he ordered Ammalat Beg to climb the steep, get as near as possible to the picket, see how many men were stationed there, and strike his steel upon the flint as many times as there were men.

Ammalat Beg turned away and disappeared into the night.

Meanwhile Djemboulat wormed along like a snake up the slope of the mound.

The Cossack was dozing. He seemed conscious of a slight noise arising from the water-side, and gazed uneasily in the direction of the river.

Djemboulat was only three steps away from him: he was lying on his stomach behind a bush.

"The cursed ducks!" muttered the Cossack, who had come to the Terek from the banks of the Don, "they are in good spirits even at night; they flutter and frolic in the water like the elves of Kiev."

On the other hand, at this moment Ammalat Beg had attained a point from which he commanded the knoll.

There were two Cossacks: one was asleep wrapped in his bourka, the other was supposed to keep awake.

Ammalat Beg clicked the steel twice upon the flint.

The sound and the sparks drew the Cossack's attention.

"Oh! oh!" said he, "what is that? Wolves, perhaps; their jaws snap, and their eyes glitter!"

And he faced about, the better to see.

Just then he thought he saw a man's figure through the darkness.

He opened his mouth to cry, "To arms!" but the cry was stayed on his lips, — Djemboulat's kandjiar was plunged to the hilt in his breast.

He fell without a moan.

The other Cossack did not even wake, and passed without knowing it from sleep unto death.

The post was wrenched out and thrown with its cask into the river.

It was a breach through which the bulk of the troops passed and overran the district.

The raid was complete and wholly successful. All peasants attempting resistance were killed on the spot. The rest hid themselves or fled. A large number of prisoners were taken, both men and women.

The Kabardians entered the houses, took everything they could find, and carried off all that was transportable; but they did not burn villages, nor devastate fields, nor spoil vineyards.

"Why touch God's gifts and man's labor?" said they. "That would be the work of brigands instead of noble mountaineers."

In an hour's time all was over for the inhabitants within a radius of three leagues.

But all was not over for the plunderers.

The call to arms had echoed all along the border; a shepherd had started the alarm.

He had been killed, but too late.

A great circle had been formed about the loose horses

ranging over the steppe, and those forming it collected the entire herd.

A Tchetchen horseman headed the band on an excellent horse, and darted off at a gallop.

Every horse whinnied, flung his tail, shook his mane to the wind, and set off in the train of the Tchetchen. He led the entire band to the Terek, passed between two pickets, and plunged into the stream on his horse.

All the rest of the horses followed in his wake.

They were seen to pass like shadows; the sound of their plunge into the water was heard, and that was all!

VII.

At sunrise the fog lifted, uncovering a grand but dreadful spectacle.

A large troop of riders were returning to the mountain, dragging behind them their prisoners, some of whom were tied to the stirrups, some to the saddle, others to the horses' tails.

The hands of all were bound.

Tears and groans of despair were mingled with shouts of triumph.

Laden with spoils, hindered by the slow pace of the herds of cattle, the raiders were making their way to the Terek. The princes, nobles, and picked horsemen rode gayly along as escort, leading and flanking the cortege.

But, in the distance and from all directions, the border Cossacks began to appear, skulking behind trees and hiding behind bushes.

The Tchetchens sent out sharp-shooters, and the fighting began.

On all sides gunshots blazed and flashed.

The vanguard pushed on, driving the herds before, and forcing them to swim the river.

But clouds of dust were then seen rising behind them.

It was the storm.

Six hundred mountaineers, led by Djemboulat and Ammalat Beg, stopped their horses and faced about to give the others time to cross the river.

With no attempt at order they charged the Cossacks at full speed, yelling as they rode, though not a gun was taken from behind the back, not a sword gleamed in a horseman's hand.

The Tchetchens have a way of handling their weapons only at the last moment.

But at twenty paces from the Cossacks they brought their guns to their shoulders and fired; then they swung the guns behind their backs, and drew their schaskas

But, even while responding with a lively fusillade, the Cossacks drew rein, whirled, and fled.

Spurred on by their eagerness for a fight, the mountaineers started in pursuit. The fugitives led them on towards a wood.

In this wood the soldiers of the Forty-third Regiment were lying in ambush.

They formed a square, lowered their bayonets, and fired on the Tchetchens.

In vain did the latter leap down from their horses and endeavor to penetrate the forest in order to attack the Russians in flank and rear.

The artillery joined in with its boom.

Kotzarev, the dread of the Tchetchens, the man whose bravery was most noted among them, commanded the Russian troops.

From that time forward, there was no doubting the outcome. Three successive volleys of artillery dispersed the mountaineers, who retraced their course toward the river.

But on the bank of the Terek, raking the course of the stream, a masked battery had been stationed.

It opened fire.

The canister burst in the thickest of their flight.

At every shot several horses, struck dead, rolled over in the stream, dragging down their riders and drowning them.

It was fearful, then, to see the prisoners, bound to the horses, unable to help themselves, and exposed like their conquerors to the Russian fire.

The old Terek, reddened with blood, received all, friends and enemies, within its cold waves, tossing the bodies of men and animals and sweeping all, living and dead, toward the sea.

Waiting to the last, covering the retreat, and struggling like lions against the soldiers, Djemboulat and Ammalat Beg with a hundred horsemen guarded the crossing, charging the Russian infantry who came within reach, swooping down on the border Cossacks, returning to their comrades, and encouraging them by word and deed; and finally, they also, last of all, plunged into the Terek, and crossed.

Upon reaching the opposite bank, they leaped from their horses, and, guns in hand, stood ready to dispute the passage of the Russians, who, crowding on the bank, made a feint of clearing the river in turn.

But, meanwhile, two versts below the place where they were joining battle, a large body of Cossacks had crossed the Terek and taken up a position between river and mountain.

Their echoing shouts, joyous and triumphant, behind the Tchetchens, alone revealed their presence.

The destruction of the mountaineers was inevitable.

Ammalat Beg took in the situation at a glance.

"Well, Djemboulat," said he, "all is over, and our fate is decided. Do what you will yourself; as for me, the Russians shall not have me alive: it is better to die by the bullet than the rope!"

"And I," said Djemboulat,—"think you my hands are made for chains? Allah forbid! The Russians may have my body; my soul, never!"

Then, remounting his horse and standing in the stirrups, he cried, —

"Comrades, fate is against us, but our steel is left. Let us sell our lives dearly to the unbelievers. The conqueror is not he who wins the battlefield, but he who wins glory; and glory belongs to him that prefers death to captivity."

"We will die! we will die!" shouted the mountaineers in chorus.

"And let our good horses die with us, and when dead serve us as a rampart," said Djemboulat.

And, leaping from his horse, he drew his sword and, setting the example, stabbed him in the throat.

Every mountaineer did the same, while yelling defiance at the Russians.

A great ring of dead horses encircled the Tchetchens.

Then each man crouched behind his horse with loaded gun.

Seeing what a terrible defence the mountaineers were prepared to make, the Cossacks paused, hesitating as to whether they ought to attack men in such desperate straits.

And then a voice rang out upon the silence; a Tchetchen was chanting the death-song.

The voice was firm, vibrant, ringing; and the Russians could hear the song from the first word to the last.

> "Glory be ours! Disgrace to the foe!
> Better to die than shame to know."

All the doomed men repeated in chorus, —

> "Glory be ours! Disgrace to the foe!
> Better to die than shame to know."

Then the solo voice continued. —

" Oh, weep, fair dames, on mountain-side,
And to our hearts give sigh for sigh,
For, thinking of sweetheart and bride,
Your mountaineers are now to die.
For this, the sleep that meets the brave
Is not the sleep that sweet life gave
Mid songs of joy and lullaby.
No, 't is the dreary sleep that bids
The rock or clod that weights our lids,
While tempests thunder in the sky.

" But, no; weep not, ye sweet brides, so.
The houris green, your sister things,
Will come with eyes that catch the glow
Of morning-stars through heaven that go,
And take us hence on white, white wings.

" Nay, mother, gaze not up the road,
Put out the fire, then seek thy bed ;
In vain thy heart its ill doth bode, —
Dear mother, none wait for the dead.
Seek not thy neighbor of the plain,
And say, to lull thy bitter pain,
' My son will come to-morrow, and —'
Thy son is on the hill at rest :
His heart is broken in his breast,
His sword is broken in his hand.

Chorus.

" Glory be ours ! disgrace to the foe !
Better to die than shame to know.

" Weep not vain tears ; though life be done.
Oh, mother, I avenged have died :
Thy milk, while in my veins it run,
To lion's blood had changed its tide.
And never in the hottest fight
Did thy son e'er in coward fright

Hear voice of fear in counsel deep.
He falls with hands nor clasped nor bound,
He falls at last on brave men's ground,
And here he sleeps his last long sleep.

" The rill that runs from mountain height
In spring, soon dries its waters pure;
The dawn that heralds morning's light
Wears robes all flowery-hued and bright, —
Her realm and rule an hour endure.
Oh, comrades, now we 'll make our prayer,
We go no farther on our way,
But like the brooklet, once so fair,
We cease, and fade like dawn of day.

" Yet we, at least, shall pass in wrath
And leave behind the tempest's path
Which stains the heavens with redness dire;
On flowers, on sands we 'll leave a trace
That time nor storm shall e'er efface,
The stains of blood and smoke and fire.

Chorus.

" Glory be ours! disgrace to the foe!
Better to die than shame to know."

Struck by the solemnity of the scene before their eyes, Cossacks and soldiers listened respectfully to the death-song of twelve hundred brave men.

At last the signal was given: a mighty huzza burst from the Russian ranks.

The Tchetchens responded with a death-like silence.

But when the Russians were no more than twenty paces from them, they rose; each sighted his man, and at the order, " Fire!" given by Djemboulat and Ammalat Beg, a wreath of flame enveloped the beleaguered men.

Then, breaking his gun, every man sent up a war-cry as he drew his schaska with the right hand, and his kandjiar with the left.

Three times did the Russians assail the bloody fortification, three times were they repulsed.

The fourth time, they gathered their forces for a final effort; during ten minutes longer, like a great serpent coiled in a circle, flashed the sabres and kandjiars counterfeiting its scales.

At last the gigantic reptile was broken into three or four pieces. The conflict became terrible. A hand-to-hand struggle ensued. Fountains of blood gushed forth amidst curses and death-shrieks.

The abrecks, that they might not become separated in the fray, bound themselves together with their girdles. None asked for mercy, none demanded quarter.

All fell under the Russian bayonets.

A small group was still on their feet and still fought on.

In the centre of this group, like two Titans, stood Djemboulat and Ammalat Beg.

For one instant the Russians recoiled before that hopeless defence, and made a pause.

"On!" cried Djemboulat, leading his last onset. "On, Ammalat Beg! Death is liberty!"

But Ammalat Beg was deaf to the last call of the Tchetchen chief. A blow on the head from the butt of a gun had stretched him senseless on the ground, covered with the dead and steeped in gore.

VIII.

COLONEL VERKOVSKY to his fiancée, Marie N , al Smolonsk: —

DERBEND, Oct. 7, 1819.

Two months! — It is a very brief period in the common course of life; but to me, the two months that have just rolled by, my darling Marie, are two centuries. Two centuries ago, then, instead of two months ago, I received your dear letter.

During that time the moon has revolved twice around the earth.

There is a past which I recall with pleasure; there is a future into which I plunge with hope; but, away from you, with no news of you, there is no present. The Cossack who brings the post appears; he holds a letter in his hand. I spring up, recognize your writing, break the seal, kiss the lines penned by your dear hand. I devour the thoughts dictated by your pure heart. I am happy, I have left the earth, I am in heaven! But scarcely have I closed your letter before ill-boding thoughts invade my mind. That is all well, doubtless, but all that is in the past, and is, perhaps, no longer, even now. Is she well, the one for whom I would give my life? Does she love me as well to-day as yesterday? Will the happy time ever come when we shall be reunited, never to part again; when there shall be for us neither separation nor distance; when the expressions of our love shall not become chilled in passing from heart to paper? Or, before that time shall come, alas! will not the letters themselves have grown cold? Will not the fire which burns on the altar of her heart have gone out, dying little by little? Pardon all these fears, my love; they are the growths which flourish on the soil of absence. With my heart near yours, I believe everything; away from you, on the contrary, I doubt everything. You bid me take you into my life, to tell you what I do, what takes place around me in this little vortex of which I am the centre; what I think, how I busy myself, even from hour to hour, from minute to minute. It has forced me to endure again all the pangs which I have just described, hard-hearted being, who will that I shall not only suffer, but analyze my sufferings, tear my wounds!

However, you command, I obey.

My life is the imprint of a chain on the sand. My service, if not amusing, by its fatigue helps at least to pass the time. I am thrown into a frightful climate which no constitution can withstand, into the midst of a fellowship which stifles my soul. I no longer find among my associates the only one who could have understood me, nor any one among the Asiatics with whom to share a sentiment. Everything about me is so wild that I bruise myself on everything I touch; so narrow that I seem to breathe the air of a dungeon. Warmth could more easily be drawn from an iceberg than a glow of enjoyment from this accursed country.

I will give you a detailed account of my last week It is the most interesting and the liveliest of all that I have spent in the City of the Iron Gates.

I recall having written you that we were returning, with the Governor-General of the Caucasus, from the expedition upon Akoutcha. We succeeded off-hand; Shah Ali Khan fled into Persia. We burned a dozen villages with the hay and corn; we flayed, spitted, and roasted the enemy's sheep. Finally, when the snow forced the in habitants to come down from the cliffs, they surrendered and gave hostages; after which, we returned to the fortress of Bounaıa. There, our division was obliged to break up for the winter, and my regiment has come back to its quarters in Derbend.

The next day the general was compelled to leave us to enter upon a second expedition on the border. Consequently, there was a great throng of people anxious to take leave of their well-beloved chief. Alexis Petrovitch left his tent and came to us. Who does not know his face, if not from life, at least from portraits? I do not know of such another in existence, another so expressive as his.

A poet once wrote of him: —

"Fly, Tchetchen, fly! The man whose word
In vain was never known to warn,
Is roused; his rally-cry is heard,
His order passed : 'We march the morn!'
The whistling ball that carries death
Takes but the heaving of his breath.
His shout's the cry the mighty saith,
It is the thunder of the fight.
He bends his brow with love or hate
Of friends or foes, and names their fate ;
And where he points, or soon or late,
Death rushes on, nor stays his might."

And the poet has not said too much.

You should see his coolness in battle, his ease on his reception day! Sometimes he strews before the Asiatics the garlands of his flowery speech, as full of imagery as Persian poetry; sometimes he routs them, pursues, and crushes them with a single word. In vain do these demons of deceit endeavor to hide their most secret plans in the recesses of their hearts; his eye penetrates them, and a week, a month, a year beforehand, he will tell them what they intend to do. It is amusing to see how a man of guilty conscience turns white and red under the torture of his steady, piercing eye, and how readily the same eye discerns merit wherever it is to be found, rewards it with a smile, and how, with a word that goes straight to the heart, he repays courage and loyalty.

May God grant to every brave soldier the glory and happiness of serving under such a leader!

It is curious to note his relations in his own house with those who serve under him. It is a study for the observer. Every man distinguished by courage, spirit, or any talent whatever, has free entrance and full swing. There is no more rank, no more etiquette. Each has a right to say whatever enters his mind, to do as he pleases. Alexis Petrovitch [1] talks and laughs with each as a friend, advising and instructing him like a brother.

We were, then, in camp. It was last Tuesday, at teatime. His aide-de-camp had induced him to read Napoleon's campaign in Italy, that poem of the military art, as he calls it. Surrounding him, we praised, criticised, and discussed it. The great captain who, like Hannibal and Charlemagne, had crossed the Alps, would have been satisfied with the remarks and even with the criticisms of one who had so long disputed with him the great redoubt of Borodino. After tea, the reading finished, we engaged in gymnastics, we ran races and leaped ropes and ditches. we tested our strength in all sorts of exercises; the company was good, the view was magnificent. Our camp was near Tarki, overlooked by the fortress of Bournaïa.

[1] The author has intended to portray the brave general, Yermolof, the senior and the model of Russian officers.

Behind the fortress the sun was setting. At the foot of the cliff was the chamkal's house, and farther away, on the steepest slope, lay the town. Beyond all, to the east spread the vast steppe, and beyond the steppe stretched the blue expanse of the Caspian Sea. Tartar begs, Tchetchen princes, Cossacks from every river in Russia, hostages from every mountain, and the officers of all our regiments, formed a most curious and picturesque scene in which uniforms, tchokas, and coats of mail were mingled. The singers, dancers, and musicians made a group apart, and the soldiers took their share in the fête a few hundred paces below, their shakoes jauntily perched over one ear.

The conversation turned on the quality of the different poniards of the Caucasus. Each vaunted his own as made by the best blade-smith. Captain Betovitch, who had a kandjiar purchased at Andrev and mounted at Kouba, laid a wager that he could pierce three roubles placed one on top of the other.

The bet was taken; three roubles were stacked up on a block, and, left-handed though he is, Betovitch pierced the three roubles.

Just then, a frightened buffalo dashed into the midst of the musicians, and to the great delight of the on-lookers, created utter confusion. They scattered in all directions, dodging and leaping out of his way, and enraging him by their screams as they endeavored to escape.

The furious animal aimed for the group where General Yermolof was standing. Some of the officers drew their swords, others their poniards, and placed themselves in front of the lieutenant-governor; but, brushing them all aside, he drew his schaska and stationed himself in the animal's path.

The buffalo doubtless thought that he had met a worthy adversary, and bounded towards him.

With the agility of a young man, the general lightly avoided the animal; but, in the very act of springing aside, his arm was uplifted, something was seen to flash like lightning, and, while the buffalo's head, detached from the shoulders by a single blow, fell at the general's feet and remained stuck in the earth by its horns, the body by its own impetus continued three or four paces in its course, and fell, gushing forth a torrent of blood.

A great cry of astonishment and admiration arose from the spectators.

All the officers gathered about the general, — some examining the animal's head, others its body.

"A terrible sword your Excellency has there," said Captain Betovitch.

"It is worthy of going with your poniard, captain," returned the general.

And he presented him the sword.

The captain hesitated to accept it.

"Take it, take it," said Yermolof; "it is yours."

And he gave him, as he would have given an ordinary sword, that schaska whose blade alone had cost three or four hundred roubles, and whose sheath was worth as much more merely for its weight in silver.

They were still talking about this prodigious feat when an officer of the border Cossacks was announced to the general, coming on behalf of Colonel Kotzarev.

The officer entered, and presented a report.

"Permit me, gentlemen?" said the general, as if he were among his equals.

And that is the admirable side of this man: he constantly raises you to his own level, without descending to yours.

You may suppose that the permission was granted.

He read the report, accompanying its reading with a slight undertone of approval.

Then he said aloud, —

"Gentlemen, I have good news: there is a cross of St. George for one of our brave officers."

We drew near with interest.

"Well, it seems that Kotzarev has exterminated a dozen or fifteen hundred mountaineers. The bandits had crossed the Terek and devastated a village; but Kotzarev has met and overpowered them, and he sends me five prisoners; these are all that remain of their band."

Then, turning to the Cossack officer, he said, —

"Bring me a few of those gentlemen; I'll wager that some of my acquaintances are among the rogues."

They were brought before him; at sight of them his brows knit in a frown.

"Wretches!" said he, "this is the third time that you have been caught, and twice you have been released on an oath never to engage in your plundering again. What do you lack? Pastures? — you have them; flocks? — you have them; safety? — am I not here to secure it for you? — Take them away, and let them dangle from their own ropes. However, they themselves shall choose one of their number who shall be set at liberty after he has witnessed the execution, that he may carry an account of it to his comrades."

Four men were led away: a fifth remained.

He was a Tartar beg; not until then did we notice him; our whole attention had been absorbed by the others.

He was a young man of twenty-three, of marvellous beauty and with the figure of the Apollo Belvedere.

He was awaiting his turn in an attitude of supreme grace and regal pride.

As the general's eye rested upon him, he bowed and resumed his first attitude.

On his face could be read that perfect resignation to fate which is the virtue of the Mussulman.

The general's glance, charged with threatening wrath, fell upon him; but the prisoner's face underwent no change; he did not even lower his eyes.

"Ammalat Beg," the general at length said, after a moment's silence that had seemed a long time to those whose curiosity formed their sole interest in the proceedings, — "Ammalat Beg, do you remember that you are a Russian subject, that you live under the Russian laws?"

"I have not forgotten it," replied Ammalat Beg; "and if they had defended my rights, I should not to-day be standing like a culprit before you."

"You are both unjust and ungrateful," returned the general. "You and your father have made war on the Russians. If a similar thing had happened during a reign of the fathers of the caliphs from whom you pretend to have descended, your family would not now be in existence. But our emperor is so good that instead of hanging you, he gives you a government. How have you repaid his kindness? By open revolt. But that is not your greatest offence, even: you received into your house an enemy of Russia; you allowed him to assassinate a Russian officer and two soldiers in your presence, and yet, if you had repented, I should have pardoned you, in consideration of your youth and your customs; but no, you fled into the mountains and, with Ackmeth Khan, you have attacked a Russian post. Over and above all that, you became one of Djemboulat's chiefs.

and with him have just pillaged the lands of your former friends. I need not say what fate awaits you, need I?"

"No, for I know it," answered Ammalat, quietly; "I shall be shot."

"No, a ball bestows too noble a death for me to let you die by a ball!" answered the enraged Yermolof. "No! a cart shall be set with its shaft in the air, to the shaft a rope, and to the rope your neck."

"It is quite the same thing," replied Ammalat Beg, "although not the shortest death. Yet," he continued, "I have a favor to ask: since I am condemned beforehand, do not take the trouble to give me a trial. The trial will not last long, I know, but it always causes delay."

"Agreed," answered the general.

Then, turning to his aids, he said, —

"Remove him, and to-morrow let all be over."

He was led away.

The fate of this young man, so proud, so calm, so resigned, touched all. Everybody pitied him, and the more sincerely because they well knew it was impossible to save him, — an example being necessary, and Yermolof's decisions being irrevocable.

No one dared to plead for the unfortunate youth.

Each went his way.

I noticed that the general was gloomy as he returned home. I, knowing his heart, told myself that perhaps he was sorry that no one had opposed his decision.

I resolved to attempt it.

I went to head-quarters ten minutes after he had returned.

He was alone, his elbow resting upon the table. On the table lay the report which he was making to the emperor.

Alexis Petrovitch has, as you know, a great friendship for me; I am one of his intimates: he was not surprised, therefore, at seeing me.

On the contrary, he seemed to have been expecting me, for he said with a smile, —

"I think, André Ivanovitch, that you have a favor to ask. Ordinarily you come here as if you were marching to battle; but to-day one would suppose that you were treading the air, like the Mignon of your favorite poet. I will wager that you have come to ask pardon for Ammalat?"

"In faith! you have guessed right, your Excellency," I answered.

"Sit down there and let us talk this matter over," said he.

Then, after a moment's silence, he continued, —

"I know that I am said to regard the lives of men as so many playthings, and that the blood of these mountaineers is no more esteemed by me than the water that flows from their mountains. The cruellest conquerors hide their cruelty under a semblance of forbearance; while I, on the contrary, have the false reputation of a merciless man. My name ought to guard our frontiers more surely than chains and fortresses. It is expedient that all these Asiatics know my word to be as inexorable as death. One can persuade the European, move him by kindness, touch him by clemency; the Asiatic, never. To pardon him is more than a weakness, it is a crime; that is why I show them no mercy. I am cruel out of humanity: the prospect of certain punishment alone can guarantee the Russians against death, and prevent treason among the Mussulmans. Among all these people who appear to submit, there is not one who is not concealing wrath, who is not plotting vengeance. My predecessors have said and my successors will say: 'Every time that the death-sentence is in question, I would like with all my heart to pardon. I have the greatest desire to show mercy; but, judge for yourself: can I do it?' Then they shed some tears over the victim. That is all sham, my dear fellow! The laws exist, they must be executed. Lives are intrusted to me, and I must watch over them. I never talk in that way, I never shed such crocodile tears; but, every time that I sign a death-warrant, my heart weeps tears of blood."

Alexis Petrovitch was moved. He rose, took several turns about his tent, reseated himself, and continued,—

"Ah well, never has the necessity for punishment seemed more cruel than it has seemed to-day. One that has remained as long among the Asiatics as I ought not to pay any more attention to a handsome face than to a letter of recommendation. But, mark you, the face, figure, voice, and bearing of this Ammalat Beg has made a strong impression on me. I pity him."

"A good heart is worth more than intellect, general," said I, "and you are fortunately gifted: you have both."

"The heart of a public man, my dear fellow, should ground arms to his intellect. I know very well that I can pardon Ammalat: it rests with me; but I know also that I must punish him. Daghestan is filled with our enemies; Tarki, but half subdued, is ready to rise with the first puff of wind from the mountains; we must cut short all of that by a few executions, and show the Tartars that all must bow down before the Russian laws, even mercy. If I pardon Ammalat, there will be but one cry: 'Yermolof fears the chamkal!'"

"Yes," I answered; "but since we are not to follow the impulses of the heart, but to consider and reflect, do you not think that the gratitude of Ammalat's family would have great weight in the country?"

"The chamkal is an Asiatic like the rest, my dear colonel," interrupted Yermolof, "and he will be enchanted if this claimant to the principality no longer exists. No, in this entire affair, I am the least concerned in the world about his relatives."

Seeing this sort of hesitancy on the part of the governor-general, I pursued more bravely.

"Require me to perform triple service," said I; "give me no leave this year, and grant me a pardon for this young man. He is young, and Russia may find in him a good and brave servant. I make myself responsible for him."

Alexis Petrovitch shook his head.

"Listen," said he, "it is sad to relate, but it is a philosophical observation of mine, and one that assails neither God nor Providence: rarely have I done a good deed of this kind that has turned out well, and, mind you, they have not been common."

"Try it once more, general, and give us your word that if it turns out badly, this shall be the last."

"Very well! you wish it, — I pardon him; although I was only waiting for a petition like yours to excuse me in my own eyes. I pardon him unconditionally. It is not my custom, when I have yielded the main point, to haggle over details. But remember one thing: you have said that you will be responsible for him."

"Entirely. I will take him to my quarters, and be personally answerable for him, general."

"Never trust him, and remember the old story of the viper warmed in the bosom of the compassionate man. Oh, the Asiatics, the Asiatics! one day you will know them, Verkovsky; God grant it may never be at your own expense!"

I was so delighted that instead of replying to the general, or thanking him in the least, I ran to the tent where Ammalat Beg was held.

Three sentinels stood guard over him; a lighted lantern was hanging from the centre. I went in. He was so deep in his own thoughts that he failed to hear me.

I drew near enough almost to touch him; he was lying on his bourka, weeping.

That did not surprise me; it is not a cheerful prospect, to die at twenty-three.

The tears that I had just surprised gave me great pleasure: they showed the value of the pardon I brought.

"Ammalat," said I in Tartar, "Allah is great and the *serdar* is good: he grants you life."

The young man sprang to his feet; he tried to speak, but it was some time before he could utter a word, he was so overcome.

"Life? He grants me life?"

Then with a bitter smile,—

"I understand," he added; "for a man to die slowly in a gloomy prison, or, when he is accustomed to the Oriental sun, to be sent to languish amid the snows of the north, to be buried alive, separated from his relatives, his friends, his mistress; to be deprived of speech with others, and forbidden to complain to himself: that is called life; that is the pardon granted to the condemned. If that is the pardon I am granted, if that is the alternative I am given, say that I do not want such a pardon."

"You deceive yourself, Ammalat," I answered. "The pardon is entire, unconditional, without restrictions. You remain master of your estates, your actions, your will. Here is your sword; the general returns it to you, confident that you will henceforth draw it only on the side of the Russians. You shall live with me until the whole unhappy affair is forgotten, and you shall be my friend, my brother."

The idea was new to an Asiatic. He looked at me: two great tears rolled from his eyes.

"The Russians have vanquished me quite!" he cried. "Pardon me, colonel, for having thought so badly of you all. From this hour, I become a loyal subject of the Russian emperor, and my heart and sword are his. Oh, my sword! my sword!" he added looking affectionately at the blade; "let my tears wash away the Russian blood and the Tartar naphtha![1] When and how can I thank you for life and liberty?"

I am sure, dear Marie, that, for this affair, you will keep for me one of your sweetest kisses. Besides, in acting as I did, I had no thought but of you. "Marie will be pleased," I said to myself; "Marie will reward me." But when shall I claim my reward, my darling? Your mourning must still last nine months longer, and the general has refused my leave, reminding me that I renounced it myself when demanding Ammalat's life.

The fact is that my presence is necessary to the regiment. Barracks are being constructed for our winter-quarters, and if I leave the work will stop. Therefore, I remain: but my heart! my poor heart!

We have now been three days in Derbend; Ammalat is with me. He says nothing. He becomes more morose, and more barbarous day by day, but he interests me only the more. He speaks Russian well, but by rote. I am teaching him the alphabet; he progresses wonderfully. I hope to make a fine scholar of him.

[1] The Tartars give a blackish tint to the blades of their swords and poniards by dipping them in naphtha.

IX.

THE thoughts of Ammalat Beg translated from the Tartar:[1] —

Either I have been asleep heretofore, or to-day I am dreaming. There is, then, a new realm called thought. A beautiful, grand, magnificent world which has long been as unknown to me as the Milky Way, which is composed, I am told, of millions of stars. I seem to be climbing up the mountain of science out of the night and the fog; but day breaks, and the fog vanishes. With every step my horizon becomes brighter and broader. With every step I breathe more freely. I gaze at the sun, it forces me to lower my eyes; but already the clouds are under my feet. Cursed clouds! On earth you hinder me from seeing heaven; in heaven you hinder my sight of the earth.

Why is it that these simple questions, *why* and *how*, never before presented themselves to my mind? The entire universe, with all it contains of good and ill, is reflected in my soul as in a sea or mirror; yet my soul knows no more about it than the mirror. Indeed, I remember many things; but what good does it do me? The falcon does not know why the hood is placed over his eyes; the horse does not understand why he is shod. Neither do I understand why there are mountains here

[1] These fragments were found in the room occupied by Ammalat Beg at Colonel Verkovsky's quarters.

SULTANETTA.

and steppes there; here eternal snows, there oceans of burning sand. What need have we of tempests and earthquakes? And as for you, man, the most curious of the creatures issuing from the hand of the Creator, I had never thought of following your mysterious course from the cradle to the tomb. I confess that until now I have regarded books and life in the same light, — books without comprehending their import, life without comprehending its aim. But Verkovsky has lifted the bandage from my eyes, cleared the fog from my brain; he gives me the opportunity of knowing and learning; with him I try my newly fledged wings, like the young swallow with its mother. Distance and height make me wonder still, but they do not frighten me. The time will come when I shall soar like the eagle through heaven's brilliant azure.

And yet, am I the happier since Verkovsky and his lessons have taught me to think?

Formerly, a horse, a sword, a gun afforded me a child-like joy, and now that I recognize the superiority of mind over matter, I no longer desire the things that were formerly my ambitions. Once I regarded myself seriously; once I thought myself a great man; now I am at least convinced of one thing, that I am nothing. I saw nothing back of my ancestors; all that had gone before was veiled in obscurity. It was dense night, peopled with heroes borrowed from tales and legends. The Caucasus was my horizon; but, at least, I slept tranquilly through that night. I hoped one day to become celebrated throughout Daghestan: I had chosen the mountains for the pedestal of my statue, and, behold! growing wiser, I learn from books that long before my day history had peopled my chosen stage with nations struggling for glory, with heroes whose names have resounded to the echoes of Daghestan and the entire world, and that I, forsooth, was ignorant of the very names of these nations, was unaware that such heroes had been in existence. What has become of those nations? What became of those heroes lost in the night of Time, forgotten in the dust of ages? I thought that the earth belonged to the Tartars, and lo! from a glance at a simple geographical chart, I learn that they occupy a very small portion of a very small world; that they are poor barbarians compared with the European world; that no one thinks of them, that no one knows anything of them, that no one wishes to know anything of them. No! all, all is an illusion! Kings, heroes, great men are glittering illusions; that is all.

By Mahomet! it was well worth while to wear out one's brain to arrive at such a truth!

What is the good of understanding the forces of nature and the laws by which she is governed, when my own powers are helpless to govern my soul? I can rule the sea, and I cannot curb my own tears. I can divert the thunderbolt from my roof, and I cannot keep sorrow out of my soul. I was unhappy before, when I had but my moods to torment my soul; and now, as if my moods were not sufficient, here are difficulties preying upon me as my falcons prey upon the poor birds that I begin to pity, — a thing which I had never thought of doing before. The sick man gains very little from learning his malady, when on learning it he at the same time finds out that it is incurable. My sufferings are doubled by analyzing them.

But no, I am unjust. Reading shortens the long hours of separation that seem to me like winter nights; and in gaining the ability to write my thoughts, to fix the phantoms of my imagination on paper, I gain in stoutness of heart.

Of heart or pride, I know not which.

Nay, of heart; for, some day, when I see Sultanetta again, I will show her these pages in which her name occurs more frequently than Allah's in the Koran. "These are the memories of my heart," I will say; "look: on such a day I thought of you like that; on such a night I dreamed that dream of you. From these lines you can count my tears; from these words, my sighs." Perhaps we shall laugh together over these days in which I have suffered so much; but can I think of the past when beside you, my darling Sultanetta? No, all will be blotted out before me and around me, and naught of space will be illumined save the spot on which falls the ray from your eyes. By that light my heart will soften in my breast. To forget myself near you is sweeter far than to make the whole world resound with my name.

You see plainly that it is not pride.

I read tales of love, portrayals of the passions of men and women: in the first place, not one of these heroines of romance is so beautiful in body, mind, or heart as my Sultanetta, and, as for me, I bear no moral resemblance to the men whose story I read. I envy their wit, their science, their amiability, but not their love. Their warmest love is sluggish and cold; it is like a ray of moonlight shimmering on the ice. No, I cannot think that men really love, whose love is manifested thus.

There is one thing, dear, which I must confess: in vain I ask myself what friendship is. I cannot answer. I have a friend in Verkovsky, a true, sincere, kind friend. Well, he is my friend; I feel that I cannot respond as he deserves, and I blame myself for it; but it is not in my power to do otherwise. In my soul there is no room for any but Sultanetta; in my heart, no feeling other than love.

No, I will read no more; I understand nothing it says

to me. Decidedly, I am not made to climb the ladder of science. I catch my breath at the first round, I am lost in simple difficulties, I tangle the thread instead of unwinding it. I pull and break it. I have taken the colonel's encouragement for progress. But what hinders my progress? Alas! it is what makes my life's happiness and unhappiness, — love. In everything, everywhere, I see and hear Sultanetta, and often I see and hear nothing else. To forget her a single instant would seem a crime. I should as soon wish to still the beatings of my heart. Can I live without air? Sultanetta is my light, my air, my life, my soul!

My hand trembles, my heart beats. Were I to write with my blood, it would burn the paper. Sultanetta, do you know that you are killing me? Your image follows me everywhere. The remembrance of your beauty is more dangerous to me than your beauty itself. The thought that the treasure of love which I have held in my arms is forever lost to me drowns me in despair, goads me to madness. My mind is giving way, my heart is breaking. I remember every feature of your face, every change of your expression, every movement of your arm, every curve of your bust, and your foot, that seal of love, and your lips, like ripe pomegranate, and your shoulders, mine of marble! Oh! The memory alone of your voice shakes me to the soul, like the string of an instrument near breaking. And in the night time your kiss, the kiss from which I seem to drink the springs of life, falls again upon me like dew of fire. Oh! yet one kiss like that in the chapel, a single one, Sultanetta, and then, come death!

Colonel Verkovsky had, as we have seen, observed Ammalat's sadness, and, too, he had divined its cause.

Hoping to divert him, he organized a boar-hunt, a favorite pastime of the begs of Daghestan.

At the colonel's invitation, twenty begs arrived, attended by their noukars, each disposed to do his best.

December was beginning to cover the summits of the mountains of Daghestan with snow. The swelling Caspian, unnavigable during the winter, was storming the walls of the City of the Iron Gates. Through the fog whizzed the wings of bustards; all was gloomy and dull. The misting rain falling every evening seemed like the tears of the weather itself, lamenting finer days. Old Tartars, enveloped to their noses in pelisses and bourkas, were standing about the markets.

But such dull days are fine days for hunters.

The sun had barely risen from the other side of the sea, the mullahs had scarcely called to prayer, when the colonel and his guests, Ammalat included, gathered at the north gate of Derbend, after literally wading through the mud.

The route they took is sorry enough to the eye; it is the one leading to Tarki; here and there lie a few fields of madder, then come vast Tartar cemeteries in which the graves are so crowded that they look like a forest of stakes; there are a few scattered vineyards; and beyond all lies the sea, which, at that season of the year, instead of holding a shining mirror to the sky, looked like a vast basin from which a constant fog arose. On both sides of the road enormous boulders, loosened from their bases by the violence of torrents, had rolled down and remained there in a litter, showing the unconcern of men for the cataclysms of Nature.

The huntsmen were at their posts.

On arriving, the colonel sounded three shrill, prolonged blasts from his silver-hooped hunting-horn, to which the huntsmen replied with a shout indicating that they were ready.

The hunters took their positions in line, some on horses, some on foot, and the battue began.

Boars were soon started, and the crackling of the first shots was heard.

The forests of Daghestan abound in these animals; and although the Tartars, considering them unclean, hold it a sin even to touch them, they are regarded as grand game for the chase. It is a good school of practice for both shooting and courage, as the speed of the wild boar is remarkably swift, and when wounded the mountain boar especially almost always turns upon the hunter.

The line of hunters comprising thirty shots extended over a very wide space. The boldest of the sportsmen, or those surest of their aim, chose the most isolated spots in order to share with none the glory of victory.

Colonel Verkovsky, relying on his own courage and skill, took one of these posts, deep in the forest and entirely isolated. Leaning against an oak-tree, in the centre of a sort of clearing which allowed the hunter, and likewise the boar, perfect freedom of movement, he awaited the event, which, in this country where the animal remains as wild as nature and man, is almost always a hand-to-hand struggle. Shots were heard to right and left; sometimes through copses and brushwood, the colonel could distinguish a boar passing like a flash. At last, he heard a great crackling of breaking bushes, and saw an enormous old boar heading straight for him.

The colonel fired, but the ball glanced from the animal's bony skull and wedge-shaped head. Yet, stunned for a moment by the violence of the shock, the boar stood trembling in every limb without moving backward or forward. The colonel, supposing him to be more injured than he was, left his cover and started toward him. Then the animal, not knowing before whence the blow had come, recognized his enemy, and with bristles erect and gnashing teeth he made for the colonel.

Verkovsky had a second shot; he waited.

At four paces, he pulled the trigger; only the priming smoked.

What then happened took place as swift as thought.

He experienced a violent shock that felled him to the earth; but, with the admirable coolness born of tried courage, he drew his kandjiar as he fell.

It was one of the best blades of Daghestan.

The boar spitted himself upon it, but the force of his onset wrenched the weapon from the colonel's hands.

The brute had received a terrible wound; yet, from the blood in his eye and his foaming mouth, the colonel could see that he was still full of fight.

Prostrate, disarmed, conscious from a pain in his thigh that he was already wounded, the colonel gave himself up for lost.

"Help, comrades!" he cried, without hoping to be heard.

Besides, should they hear, were they within a hundred paces, they could not reach him in time to help.

Suddenly the gallop of a horse was heard: a hunter was on the track of the boar which he seemed to be pursuing.

A shot echoed; the colonel heard a shrill whizzing, followed by the deadened sound of the ball striking a soft body.

At the same instant he felt as if a mountain had been lifted from his breast.

The boar was leaving him for a new enemy.

Verkovsky rose to his elbow; a mist was before his eyes. Yet through the mist he saw a horseman who, instead of fleeing from the boar or simply awaiting him, jumped from his horse.

Man and beast rushed upon each other and rolled together on the ground.

There was a brief space during which it would have been impossible for a painter to have given any form to this monstrous group.

Yet it seemed to the colonel that the man continued to strike after the animal was already dead.

At length the infuriated slayer stood up, covered with blood and froth and mire.

It was Ammalat Beg.

The boar's head lay beside the body, completely severed from it.

The colonel arose, and with open arms, although his blood was issuing from two wounds, he ran gratefully toward the young man.

"Don't thank me," said Ammalat Beg, spurning the boar's head and stamping it with the iron heel of his boot; "I am taking revenge. Ah! accursed! ah! unclean!" continued the youth, trampling the animal under foot, as if it could still hear and feel. "It is not all for killing my friend the beg of Tavannant. Instead of turning round, you coward! instead of attacking me, who killed your father and stabbed your mother, you continued your course to gore my benefactor, the man to whom I owe my life. Ah! accursed! ah! unclean!"

"You owe me nothing now, Ammalat, and we are quits," said the colonel; "and, accursed and unclean as he is, I trust indeed that we shall be avenged by giving him tit for tat. We will inflict the Tartar punishment on him, Ammalat Beg, — retaliation. He has attacked us with his teeth; we will eat him with ours. I hope that you will lay aside your prejudices in this instance, Ammalat, and eat your share of him."

"I would eat my share of a man, had he killed my friend," responded the savage hunter; "and the flesh of an animal with far greater excuse, were its flesh ten times forbidden!"

"And, to wash down this forbidden flesh, we will sprinkle him with forbidden liquor."

"Whatever you like, colonel; it is just as well to sprinkle my burning heart with wine as with holy water, since the holy water does it no good."

Then, pressing both hands upon his breast as if to still his heart, he gave a deep moan.

The hunt was ended, — that part of it at least.

They heard the notes of the recheat. The colonel sounded three blasts from his horn; a moment later, hunters and huntsmen were surrounding him.

In few words the colonel told what had happened; then, pointing to the boar with its head severed from the body, he said, turning to the young man, —

"It was a fine stroke, Ammalat, a brave stroke!"

"It is an Asiatic's revenge. An Asiatic's revenge is deadly!"

"Friend," said the colonel, "you have seen a Russian's revenge, a Christian's; let that be a lesson to you."

And both returned to the camp.

Ammalat Beg was distrait. Sometimes he gave no answer to Verkovsky's questions, sometimes he answered quite wide of the mark. He went along by his side, peering about in all directions as if he were expecting some one, and not even thinking to ask the colonel if his wounds were painful.

Supposing that Ammalat, like a fearless hunter, was dreaming of the chase, and being in a hurry, moreover, to return and submit his leg and thigh to the surgeon's care, Verkovsky set off at a gallop and left Ammalat to his reveries.

The young man allowed him to get beyond the hill, and then, thinking himself to be alone, he rose in his stirrups and looked in all directions.

Suddenly a horseman sprang up from the bottom of a ravine, with clothes all torn by the thorny shrub growing everywhere on the slopes of the Caucasus.

The rider made straight for Ammalat Beg.

One cry issued from both throats, —

"*Aleikoum salaam!*"

And both, leaping from their horses, threw themselves into each other's arms.

"So you are here, Nephtali!" cried Ammalat Beg; "you have seen her, you have spoken to her. Oh! I see by your face that you bring good news."

He quickly took off his jacket, all embroidered with gold, and presented it to Nephtali, saying, —

"Stay, accept this, herald of good tidings.[1] Is she alive? is she well? does she love me still?"

"In the name of Mahomet, let me get my breath," said Nephtali. "You ask me so many questions, and I in turn have so many things to say, that they crowd each other like the women in the door of the mosque when their slippers are lost."

"Well, tell everything in its place. You received my letter?"

[1] It is a Tartar custom to make a present, almost always giving a garment, to the bringer of good news. In this way I received the nicham, for having announced to the bey of Tunis his cousin's arrival at Marseilles. — A. D.

"You can see for yourself, since I am here. I received your letter, and by your desire betook myself to Khunsack. I went there so quietly and silently that I awoke not so much as a bird on my way. Ackmeth Khan is well; he is at home. He inquired anxiously about you, shook his head, and asked: 'Doesn't he need a spindle for winding off the Derbend silk?' The khan's wife, who already looks upon you as her son-in-law," — Ammalat sighed and turned his eyes heavenward, — "sends you a thousand compliments and as many little pies. I bring you the compliments, but I have thrown away the little pies, which the gait of my horse had beaten into pulp."

"May the devil eat them! And — and Sultanetta?"

"Sultanetta, dear brother," said Nephtali, sighing in turn, "Sultanetta is as beautiful as the starry sky. Only, her sky, clouded over and gloomy at first, became azure when I spoke your name, when I said that I came from you. She nearly fell upon my neck; I emptied her out a whole sack of love from you. I swore that you were dying of love for her."

"And what did she answer?"

"Nothing. She fell to weeping."

"Dear heart! dear heart! and what message did she send me?"

"Ask rather what message she did not send and I shall have done sooner. She told me to say that since your going away she has not been happy even in a dream; that her heart lies buried under the snow which only your presence, like the sun in May, can melt. If I had waited for her to finish telling me all that I was to say, and to express all her wishes, we should not have met again, my dear Ammalat, till we were gray-headed; and yet she almost chased me away because she thought

I was not hurrying fast enough, and she wished you to know immediately of all her sufferings."

"Lovely being!" addressing himself to Sultanetta as if she could have heard him. "Oh, you will never know what happiness it is for me to be near you, what martyrdom not to see you!"

"Eh, by Allah! It seems as if I were listening to her, for she said exactly the same thing, Ammalat. 'Oh, let him only return,' she sobbed, 'were it but for one day, one hour, one moment!'"

"Oh, let me see her, let me see her, and die!"

"No, Ammalat, you must see her and live. Never does a man so desire to live as when gazing at her. A single look from her doubles the circulation."

"Did you tell her why I cannot carry out the dearest of all my wishes?"

"I told her so many things that if you could have heard them you would have taken me for the poet of the Shah of Persia. She wept her eyes out over them, poor child!"

"You need not have driven her to despair, Nephtali; perhaps what cannot be done now may be done later. To banish hope from a woman's heart is to banish love. A woman without hope does not love long."

"You are wasting your breath, Ammalat; on the contrary, hope, among lovers, is an endless ball of yarn. They hardly believe in estrangement when they see it. If they love you, they believe in everything, even in ghosts! Listen, Sultanetta is positive that were you even in the grave you would come out of it to see her."

"The grave and Derbend are the same thing to me, Nephtali; my body is at Derbend, my soul at Khunsack."

"And your mind, where is that, Ammalat? It is

running at large, it seems to me. Are you so badly off with the colonel, for a man who six months ago was to have been hanged? No. You are free, you are amused, loved like a brother, treated like a betrothed. Sultanetta is beautiful, I know very well; but Verkovsky is good, and you can well sacrifice to friendship a small part of love."

"And what else am I doing, Nephtali? If you only knew what it costs me! It seems to me that what I give Verkovsky is a piece torn from my heart. Friendship is a fine thing, but it does not take the place of love. Nephtali."

Nephtali sighed.

"Have you spoken of Sultanetta to the colonel?" he asked.

"I have never dared, although a hundred times I have wished to speak; but the words stop at my lips. As soon as I open my mouth the name of Sultanetta seems to block the passage. He is so wise that I am afraid of wearying him with my folly. He is so kind that I fear to tire his patience. Imagine, Nephtali, he is in love with a woman with whom he was raised. He was to have married her; but, in 1814, during the war with France, he was thought to have been killed. The woman, who had already struggled for three years to keep her heart for Verkovsky, believing that he was dead, yielded at last, and married another man. In 1815 he returned. His Marianne was married. What do you think I would have done in his place? I would have buried my kandjiar in the perjurer's heart. I would have carried her off to possess her, were it only for an hour. No; he knew his rival to be an honorable man, as they say; he was coldblooded enough to remain his friend, and saw his former promised bride without stabbing both of them."

"A rare man," said Nephtali; "he must be a true friend."

"Yes, but what a frozen lover! Forbearing as he was, the husband was jealous. What did Verkovsky do? He went into service in the Caucasus. Fortunately or unfortunately, the husband died. Ah! now he would saddle his horse, you would think, get on his back and start. No. The governor tells him that his presence is necessary here, and he remains — not for eight days, or a month, or three months, but for a year, a century, an eternity! As for his love, he feeds it with paper every eight days, when the post comes. No, you can see, Nephtali, such a man, however good he may be, would not understand my love. There is too great a difference between our ages and especially our ideas. All that chills my friendship and keeps me from being open."

"Strange man that you are!" said Nephtali, with a degree of sadness. "You do not love Verkovsky, although, of right, he deserves your love and respect more than any other."

"Who has told you that I do not love him?" cried Ammalat, with almost a shudder. "No, no, on the contrary, I must love him as my benefactor, as the man who saved my life. Oh! I love everybody since knowing Sultanetta. I would like to cover the earth with flowers, to make the universe one great garden."

"To love everybody is to love nobody, Ammalat."

"You are wrong, Nephtali. The universe might drink from my cup of love, and my cup would still be full," said Ammalat, smiling.

"That is what comes of seeing a beautiful girl without her veil, and never afterwards seeing anything but veils and eyebrows. Like a nightingale of the Valley of Aourmès, you need a cage to make you sing."

"What is the Valley of Aourmès like?" asked Ammalat Beg.

"In the spring it is the realm of roses; in autumn, the realm of raisins," replied Nephtali.

And, as a body of belated hunters was advancing toward them, the two friends turned their horses and plunged into the depths of the wood.

X

COLONEL VERKOVSKY to his fiancée: —

DERBEND, April, 1820.

Come, dear Marie, heart of my heart! come and admire with me a beautiful night in Daghestan. Derbend, like dark-colored lava rock fallen from the crest of the Caucasus, lies peacefully on a bed of flowers; the wind wafts me the breath of the almond-trees; a nightingale is singing in the thicket behind the fortress. All things seem springing into life, all breathe of love. Nature, blushing like a modest bride, hides in a misty veil. The ocean of mist works wonders with the Caspian. Below, the sea heaves like an embossed cuirass rising with the breath of a mighty breast. Above, the fog rolls in silvery billows lighted by the full moon which is swinging in heaven like a golden lamp round which gleam the stars, diamonds strewn on the azure. Then too, every moment, the moon's fickle beams change the aspect — I will not say of the landscape: limitless fogs and a boundless sea do not constitute a landscape — of the horizon, which one might fancy to be the threshold of the kingdom of phantoms, the empire of dreams.

You cannot imagine, dear love, the sad and, at the same time, the sweet emotions inspired in me by the sight and sound of the sea. My thoughts at once dwell upon the immortality of our souls, of the infinity of our love. Love fills me and envelops me. It is the only great and immortal sentiment that man can have. It is his ocean.

In the winter of sadness, its flame keeps me warm, its light is my guide through the night of doubt; I love then without weeping, and have faith in everything. You smile at my fancy, sister of my soul; you wonder at this melancholy strain. Ah! well, to whom should I tell my thoughts, if not to you? You know that I am a sort of lantern, and the flame burning in my heart outlines all my emotions on my face, and, as you will read me with your heart and not your mind, I am not disturbed. In any case, if any points in my letters seem obscure, your happy fiancé will explain them to you in the month of August next. I cannot think without delirium of the moment when I shall see you again; I count the hours that separate us, I count the versts between. Thus, in June you will visit the springs of the Caucasus, and then only a few icy peaks of the granite chain will be between us. How many years of my life would I give to hasten the happy hour of our meeting! Our souls have so long been affianced! Why then have they been separated until now?

Our Ammalat is always reticent with me. I do not blame him; I know how difficult it is, how impossible even, to change customs absorbed with the mother's milk and the air of one's native land. Persia's despotism has imbued the soul of the Caucasian Tartars with the basest passions, has filled their hearts with the most cowardly deceitfulness. Could it be otherwise in a government based upon the exchange of a great despotism for a petty one, in which even a just trial is a rare thing, in which power is nothing but the right to commit robbery without chastisement?

"Master, do with me what you will; but allow me to do as I will with my inferiors."

That is the whole sum of the Asiatic rule.

Hence it follows that every man, finding himself between two enemies, the one who is oppressing him and the one whom he is oppressing, is accustomed to conceal his thoughts as he conceals his money. Hence every man dissembles before the powerful to obtain power, before the rich to obtain the price of persecution or denunciation. Hence, in short, the Tartar of Daghestan will not utter a word, will not take a step, will not give a cucumber without the hope of a gift in return. Churlish with whoever has neither power nor wealth, he cringes before power and crawls before wealth. He will lavish caresses on you, give you his children, his house, or his soul, in order to keep his money; and if he shows you any civility whatever, rest assured that the civility covers some speculation. In business, a *denier* will spoil a trade: it is hard to conceive the extent of their love for gain. The Armenians have a viler, more contemptible character than they; but the Tartars, I think, are more treacherous and greedy. Now, it is obvious that Ammalat, with such examples before him from his infancy, has been influenced by them, although in his nobility he has preserved a great scorn for all that is base and unworthy; but nature conferred on him a dissembling character as an indispensable weapon against his enemies, open or secret. The ties of blood, so sacred with us, do not exist among the Asiatics: the son with them is the father's slave; brother is enemy to brother. They place no confidence in their neighbor because their religion has omitted to tell them to love their neighbor as themselves. Jealousy, inspired by wife or mistress, stifles all other sentiments. There is no friendship among them. A child brought up by an enslaved mother, ignorant of a father's caress, choked by the Arabic alphabet, is secretive even with the children of his own age. From his first tooth, he goes where he will; at the first hint of a mustache, all doors, all hearts are closed to him. Husbands regard him uneasily, and drive him like a wild beast; and the first heart-throb, the first impulse of his nature are already crimes in the eye of Mohammedanism. He must let nothing of what passes within him be seen by his nearest relative, by his best friend. If he weeps, he must draw his bachlik over his eyes, and weep in silence and alone.

I tell you all this, dear love, that you may not condemn Ammalat. These Asiatic customs are so at variance with ours that they need to be explained at every turn. Thus, for nearly a year and a half of his stay with me, I did not know the name of the woman he loves, although he well understood that it was not from curiosity that I sought to learn the secrets of his heart.

At last, one day he told me all.

This is how it came about.

We were taking a ride, Ammalat and I, outside of the town; we had followed the mountain road, and, advancing farther and higher, we discovered ourselves, without having realized it, near the village of Kemmek, where the famous wall passes which used to secure Persia against invasions from the tribes that dwelt on the northern steppes of the Caucasus. The chronicles of Derbend have it that this wall was built by a certain Isfendiar. Hence comes the tradition attributing the work to Alexander the Great, who never came so far as this. In all probability, it was Nushirvan who discovered it, had it rebuilt, and stationed sentinels upon it.

Since then, it has been repaired several times; finally, for want of repairs, it has fallen into the state in which we find it to-day. The wall is said to have extended from the Caspian Sea to the Black Sea along the Caucasus, having iron gates at its terminus at Derbend, and iron gates were at its centre at the Pass of Dariel. Moreover, traces of it are seen in the mountains as far as they can be followed. They are lost sight of only over precipices and gorges. Yet, in spite of the searches that have been instituted from the Black Sea to Mingrelia, no trace of it is to be found. I looked with interest at this old wall flanked by watch-towers, and I was astonished at the greatness of the ancients, even in their caprices,— caprices to which the Orientals of to-day cannot attain. The wonders of Babylon, Lake Mœris, the pyramids of the Pharaohs, the great wall of China,— that wall carried through the wildest regions, over the crests of the highest peaks, across the deepest gorges,— testify to the giant will and boundless power of the ancient kings. Neither time nor earthquakes have been able to destroy the work of man, nor the feet of centuries to stamp out the remains of this bold antiquity.

I confess that this sight inspired me with both solemn thoughts and pride. I reviewed the work of Peter the Great, that founder of a new empire. I pictured him on the ruins of this Asiatic power, mapping Russia from its midst with his powerful hand, and adding her to Europe. How brilliant must have been the lightnings of his eyes, flashed from the Caucasus! What thoughts teemed in his brain! What inspiration swelled his breast! The prodigious future of his country stretched out before his vision, as boundless as the horizon. In the great mirror of the Caspian he saw reflected the future grandeur of Russia, planted by him, sprinkled with the dew of blood. He aimed, not to achieve foolish and brutal conquests, as these barbarians have done, but to secure the happiness of human kind. Astrakhan, Derbend, Baku, all are links of the chain by which he wished to get round the Caucasus, thereby joining the commerce of India and Russia.

Oh, Idol of the North! you whom nature created to flatter man's vanity and cause him at the same time to despair of ever attaining your height, your giant shade rises before me, and the flood of years is dashed into spray at your feet!

Pensive and silent, I continued my way.

This Caucasian Wall extends in a northerly direction, and is built with square blocks of hewn stone, fitted in with stones that are narrower and consequently longer than wide. It is what the Greeks termed the Pelasgic structure. At many points the battlements still remain; but acorns have fallen into interstices and germinated, and the slow but irresistible levers of the roots have spread the stones, and gradually caused the falling of portions of the wall that had warmed in its bosom the oaken serpents. The eagles undisturbed make their nests in the towers formerly full of soldiers; and by the waysides, bleached by time, are found the bones of wild goats brought hither by the jackals.

At many points I lost every trace of the wall; then suddenly I would see it rising again from the grass and undergrowth.

Having proceeded thus for nearly three versts, we arrived at a gate, and passed from the north side to the south under an arch covered with herbs and roots.

We had hardly gone twenty paces when we came upon six armed mountaineers.

They were lying in the shade near their horses, which were browsing on the grass.

Then I saw what a mistake I had made in taking so long a ride outside of Derbend without an escort.

It was impossible to escape by flight on account of the

rocks and brush. On the other hand, it was rash for two men to attack six. Nevertheless, I drew my pistol from its holster; but Ammalat, taking in the situation, decided at a glance, and, thrusting back my weapon into its case, said in an undertone, —

"Don't touch your pistol, or we are lost; only, don't take your eyes from me, and do what you see me do."

The brigands had seen us; they rose quickly and seized their guns.

One man only remained stretched on the grass.

Raising his head, he looked at us, and made a sign to his companions.

Instantly we were surrounded, and a mountaineer seized my horse by the bridle.

There was but one path in front of us, and the Lesghian chief was lying in the middle of that.

"I beg that you will descend from your horses, my dear guests," said he, smiling.

I hesitated. Ammalat made me a sign to remain on my horse, but he sprang to the ground.

That appeared to satisfy the Lesghian chief.

Ammalat approached him.

"Good day, my dear fellow!" he said. "On my word, I was not expecting to see you to-day; I thought the devil had made you into chislik long ago."

"Not so fast, Ammalat Beg!" returned the bandit, with a frown. "Before such a thing happens, I live in hopes of giving the eagles a few carcasses of Russians and of Tartars like yourself."

"How goes the sport?" demanded Ammalat, as tranquilly as if he had not heard.

"Badly. The Russians keep as close as cowards."

I started; but I encountered two glances fixed upon

me at the same time, — the hateful glance of the mountaineer and the gentle, serene gaze of Ammalat Beg.

"I have taken," continued the Lesghian, "only a few flocks and a dozen cavalry horses, and really I was deciding this very day that I must return empty-handed. But Allah is great, and he sends me a rich beg and a Russian colonel."

On hearing these words, my heart seemed to stop beating.

"Never sell your falcon when he is above the clouds," said Ammalat Beg, laughing, "but only when he has returned to your hand."

The brigand took up his gun and looked steadily at us.

"Ammalat," said he, "you are caught and well caught: don't think to escape me, either you or your companion. But," he added with a laugh, "perhaps you count on defending yourself?"

"Nonsense, Chemardant! Do you think we are fools enough to fight two to six? We like money very well; but far above money we value our lives. We are caught; we will pay, providing that you are not too exacting. You know, indeed, that I am an orphan. Neither has the colonel any parents."

"You have neither father nor mother; but you have your father's inheritance."

"I have nothing, for I am the prisoner of the Russians."

"If you are a prisoner, why not profit by the occasion to escape? I will set you free myself."

"There is the only man who can set me free," said Ammalat, pointing to me. "He has my word: until he gives it back to me, I shall follow him wherever he is pleased to lead me. A Mohammedan's word is as invisible as a hair of a woman's head, but it is as strong as a chain of iron."

"If you have no money, we will be content with sheep; one word to Sophyr Ali, who stayed to guard your house, will settle the matter. But don't talk to me of the colonel's poverty: I know that there is not a soldier in his regiment that would not sell the last button of his uniform to ransom him. In any case, we shall see. Allah preserve me! I am not a Jew."

"Be reasonable, Chemardant," continued the young Tartar, "and we shall not think of either defence or flight."

"I believe you, and I would prefer to have the matter settled without powder or shot."

Then, with a bantering glance, he continued, —

"How fine you have become, Ammalat! What a horse! what a gun! Show me your poniard, now. It is of Kouba make!"

"No, it was made at Kisliar," replied Ammalat.

Then, drawing the weapon from its sheath, he said, —

"The scabbard is nothing to see, look at the blade. The blade is a miracle of workmanship. On the side you can see the name of the maker; read it for yourself: 'Ali Ousta Kasanisky.'"

Ammalat held up his kandjiar before the eyes of the bandit who was endeavoring to decipher the inscription engraved on the blade.

He shot me a glance that made me shudder.

Suddenly the kandjiar flashed like lightning, and disappeared to the hilt in the Lesghian's breast.

I had guessed as much. I seized the pistol in my holster, and aimed at the head of the mountaineer holding my horse.

Seeing two of their comrades fall, the other four took to their heels.

Ammalat tranquilly set to work to despoil the dead.

"My friend," said I, shaking my head, "I do not know whether I ought to commend you for what you have just done. A ruse is always a ruse,—that is to say, a narrow, mean trick, even against an enemy."

He looked up at me in astonishment.

"Really, colonel," he exclaimed, "you are a strange man! That bandit has injured the Russians terribly. Don't you know that he would have drained our blood drop by drop to get gold?"

"True, Ammalat," I answered; "but to lie, to call him your friend, to be talking with him in friendly fashion, and suddenly plunge your kandjiar into his heart! Could we not have begun as we ended?"

"No, colonel, no, we could not. If I had not approached the chief, if I had not addressed him as a friend, we should have been killed at the first movement that we made. I know the mountaineers very well. They are brave, but only in the presence of their chief. It was necessary therefore to begin with him. When he was dead, see how they ran!"

I again shook my head.

This Asiatic deceit, to which I owed my life, did not please me.

As for Ammalat, after taking the chief's weapons, he came to secure those of the Lesghian whom I had dropped with a shot from my pistol.

To my great amazement, the poor devil was not dead. On seeing him fall, I had turned my horse away from him.

He uttered a few words that sounded like a prayer.

Ammalat approached him, and his astonishment was greater than mine on recognizing the wounded man — the ball had pierced both cheeks — as a noukar of Ackmeth Khan's.

"How do you come to be with these Lesghian brigands?" demanded he.

"The devil tempted me," he answered; "Ackmeth Khan sent me to the village of Kemmek with a letter to Ibrahim, the physician, asking him to come to Khunsack without delay."

"You were sent for Ibrahim?" demanded Ammalat, quickly.

"Yes."

"Who, then, is ill at Khunsack?"

"The young Khaness Sultanetta."

"Ill?" cried Ammalat; "Sultanetta ill?"

"Here is the letter," said the noukar.

And, upon this, he handed Ammalat Beg a little roll of money with a paper.

Ammalat became as pale as death; tremblingly he unfolded the paper, and as he read, repeated in a scarcely audible voice, —

"'She eats nothing! — For three nights she has not slept! She is delirious; her life is in danger, save her!'

"My God! my God!" cried Ammalat, "and I was laughing, amusing myself, while the soul of my soul is on the point of leaving earth! Oh! may all the curses of Allah fall on my head, if only she may be cured! Dear, beautiful girl! oh! you are drooping, withering, O rose of Avarie! Death beckons you, saying, 'Come!' and, while calling on me to save you, you are forced to follow Death! — Colonel, colonel," he cried, seizing my hand, "in the name of your God, grant my sacred prayer, the only one I will ever make you. Let me see her once, once more, a last time."

"Whom do you wish to see, Ammalat?"

"Sultanetta, the soul of my soul, the apple of my eye, the light of my life; Sultanetta, the daughter of the khan of Avarie. She is ill, dying, dead perhaps. While I waste speech here, she is dying! and I have not received her last look, her last sigh. Oh! why do not the burning ruins of the sun fall upon my head? Why does not the earth open and swallow me up?"

And he fell upon my breast, suffocated by the tears which would not come, sobbing aloud, but unable to utter another word.

It was no time to reproach him with his long-continued reticence; but was it indeed right that I should let a prisoner return, even for one day, to the house of one of Russia's greatest enemies?

There are some situations in life before which all social proprieties, all political considerations efface themselves, and Ammalat was in such a strait.

Whatever might come of it, I resolved to grant his request.

I clasped him in my arms: our tears were mingled.

"Friend," said I, "go where your heart calls you; God grant that where you go you will carry health and peace of mind! *Bon voyage*, Ammalat!"

"Adieu, my benefactor!" he cried; "adieu forever, perhaps! If God takes Sultanetta from me, he will take my life at the same time. Farewell, and Allah keep you!"

And he set off at a gallop, descending the mountain with the swiftness of a rock bounding into the valley.

As for the wounded man, I put him in the saddle, and, leading my horse by the bridle, I brought him back to Derbend.

So then, it is true: he is in love.

Yes, I understand your remonstrance, darling Marie; but Khan Ackmeth is the enemy of the Russians. Pardoned by the emperor, he has betrayed us. There is no possible alliance between Ammalat and him except by Ammalat's betraying us in his turn, or by Ackmeth Khan's deciding to remain neutral.

We cannot believe one of these things, we cannot hope for the other.

What could I do? I have suffered so much from love myself, dear Marie! I have shed so many tears upon my pillow! I have so often desired the rest of the dead, the peace of the tomb, to still my poor heart, that I cannot resist such sufferings. Ought I not to pity a young man whom I tenderly love, for loving foolishly himself? Unfortunately, my pity is not a bridge that can conduct him to happiness. Had he not been loved, perhaps he would gradually have forgotten.

Certainly, — and I seem to hear your sweet voice making this observation, — certainly circumstances may alter for them, as they have altered for us. In this world, can unhappiness alone be everlasting?

I say nothing, but I suspect — I fear for them, and, who knows! perhaps for us.

We are too happy, my dearest Marie! the future smiles upon us, hope sings its sweetest songs. But the future! It is a calm sea to-day, a stormy one to-morrow! And hope is the siren. Yes, to be sure, everything is ready for our reunion; but are we reunited?

I do not know why, occasionally a fear stabs me to the heart like cold steel. I do not know why it seems to me that this separation, so near its close, will last forever.

Oh! all this affright, all these terrors, all this anguish will disappear, have no fear, my dear love, with the very moment when I shall press your hand against my lips, your heart against my heart.

Soon, soon, my darling!

XI.

On the evening of that same day, Ammalat's horse fell under him, never to get up again.

He procured another, and continued his way without thought of food or drink. On the second day, he came in sight of Khunsack.

It was eleven o'clock in the morning. He had travelled twenty-four hours.

The farther he advanced, the stronger grew his fears.

Would he find his beloved Sultanetta alive or dead?

A chill passed through his frame as he saw the towers of the khan's palace.

He could see nothing, conjecture nothing.

"Which shall I find down there?" he asked himself,— "life or death?"

And he urged his horse with whip and knees.

A rider was preceding him, armed as for a fight; another was coming to meet that one along the road from Khunsack.

When they were within such distance as to be able to recognize each other, each pushed on at a gallop to meet the other.

Were they friends or foes?

In full career each drew his sword; on meeting, each lunged at the other.

Neither spoke a single word. Did not the sparks flying from their schaskas speak for them?

Ammalat Beg, whose way they barred, watched them in amazement.

But the combat was brief. The horseman who had come from the same direction as Ammalat Beg, fell backward upon his horse's crupper, and thence to the ground.

His head was laid open to the eyes.

The victor calmly wiped his sword, and, addressing Ammalat, said,—

"You are welcome, be my witness."

"I have witnessed the death of a man," replied Ammalat. "How can that help you?"

"The man had injured me. It was not I who killed him, but God. Your presence helps me, in that no one can say that I murdered him by lying in wait, and afterwards murder me in the same fashion. It was in combat, was it not?"

"Yes, certainly," answered Ammalat.

"And you will swear to it if need be?"

"Since it is the truth."

"Thanks; that is all I desire of you. I do not ask your name, I know it. You are the nephew of Chamkal Tarkovsky."

"But why had you quarrelled?" pursued Ammalat. "You were mortal enemies, then, to have fought so desperately?"

"We were mortal enemies, as you say. We had caught twenty sheep between us: ten belonged to me, ten to him. He was not willing to let me have mine, and he killed them all, profiting nobody; then he slandered my wife. He would have done better, the miscreant, to curse the tomb of my father, and the name of my mother, than to attack the honor of my wife. I sprang upon him with my poniard, but we were separated. Then we agreed, wherever we might meet, to fight it out to the death. We have met: he is dead,

Allah has maintained the right. — You are going to Khunsack, probably, to visit the khan?" queried the horseman after a moment's silence.

"Yes," answered Ammalat, leaping his horse over the dead man's body.

"The visit is untimely, Beg," admonished the other, shaking his head.

Ammalat's blood surged to his heart. He nearly fell from his horse.

"Has any misfortune overtaken the house of Khan Ackmeth?" he demanded.

"His daughter Sultanetta was very ill."

"And — she is dead?" cried Ammalat, losing his color.

"Perhaps so. An hour ago, when I passed the house, every one was running about. On the stairs and through the hall the women were weeping as if the Russians had taken Khunsack. In any case, if you wish to see her alive, make haste."

But Ammalat heard no more, he had set off at a run, only the dust was to be seen rising from his horse's hoofs. He cleared the hill still between him and the village, tore through the streets, dashed into the court, leaped from his horse, and, all breathless, bounded up the flight of steps, and on to Sultanetta's chamber, brushing aside everything and every one that he encountered on his way, noukars and servants, and, almost senseless, fell on his knees at Sultanetta's bedside.

Ammalat's unexpected arrival drew an exclamation from all who were in the room.

At this exclamation Sultanetta, pale, dying, with life already almost extinct, gave a start in the depths of her delirium. Her cheeks burned with a deceptive tint. Like the autumn leaf which reddens and falls, her eyes bright ened with the last glow of the departing soul. For several hours now, overcome by her weakness, she had been motionless and speechless; but, amidst all the exclamations, she had recognized the voice of Ammalat.

Life, so near its flight, hesitated, like the trembling flame of a candle steadying itself at the moment when we think it is going out.

She rose on one arm; her eyes shone.

"Is it you?" she murmured, extending her hands to Ammalat.

"She speaks! she speaks!" cried Ammalat.

And every one stood open-mouthed and with breath suspended.

"Allah be praised!" she continued, "I die content, I die happy."

This time, there rose a cry of despair; they thought her dead.

A smile sealed her lips; her eyes were closed, she had again lost consciousness.

In despair Ammalat took her in his arms; he listened neither to the khan's questions nor to his wife's reproaches.

Force was employed to wrest him away and banish him from the room. Crouching at the door, prostrating himself on the floor, sobbing, at times beseeching Allah to save Sultanetta, at times blaming heaven and upbraiding himself for the illness of his loved one, his grief, untempered by Christian resignation, was terrible to witness; it was that of the tiger, with its threatening roar.

What should have killed the sick one, saved her.

What the science of the mountain physician could not do, chance accomplished. A violent shock was needed to set in motion the frozen current of life; she would have died not so much from the malady as from the

SULTANETTA. 131

exhaustion following it, like a lamp flickering out for want of air, rather than from the violence of the wind.

At last youth gained the mastery. That violent transport had awakened life in the depths of the dying girl's heart, and, after a long, calm sleep, she awoke, in possession of a part of her lost strength, and a freshness of feeling which she had never hoped to experience again.

Her mother was leaning over her bed, waiting for r sign of recognition. Ammalat was concealed by the tapestry of the doorway; he had given his word not to enter, and the khan was standing behind him for fear that he would forget.

Sultanetta breathed a sigh, her eyes wandered vaguely around; then her glance was arrested, became fixed, and concentrated itself upon her mother.

She smiled before speaking.

"Oh, mother," she said, "it is you. If you knew how light I feel! Am I poised on wings? How sweet it is to sleep after long wakefulness, to rest after great fatigue! How fair the day is! How brilliant the light! How beautiful the sun! The very walls of the room seem to be smiling on me. Oh, I have been very ill, a long time ill, have I not?"

And with a sigh, while passing her hand over her forehead still damp with perspiration, she continued,—

"Oh, I have suffered so much. Now, glory be to Allah! I am only weak; but I feel that this exhaustion will very quickly pass away. One would think that a string of pearls was coursing my veins. Oh, how strange it is! I see all that has happened as if through a mist. I dreamed that I was plunged into an ice-cold sea and yet was burning with thirst. Then, afar off through the haze, I saw two stars. But they wavered, grew darker and darker, and threatened to go out; I kept sinking, drawn down more deeply by an irresistible force. Suddenly a voice called my name, and I felt a hand, stronger than the hand of death, raising me out of that cold, gloomy abyss. Then, in a first ray of light, I saw the face of Ammalat appear. At once the stars became more brilliant, and a flash, like a serpent of fire, struck me to the heart. Then I seemed to faint away, for I remember nothing more."

Ammalat, with bursting heart, his cheeks bathed in silent tears, and eyes and hands raised to heaven, was listening; and as he listened, he murmured a heartfelt prayer of thankfulness.

He started to rush headlong into the room when the young girl spoke his name.

But Ackmeth Khan, as much moved as he, and weeping also, said in a whisper, —

"To-morrow, to-morrow."

The next day, indeed, Ammalat was permitted to see the invalid.

Ackmeth Khan himself took him in, thus acquitting himself of his promise.

"May all the world be as happy as I," said he.

Sultanetta had been forewarned; but her emotion was none the less profound when her eyes met those of Ammalat, whom she loved so much and for whom she had so long waited.

The lovers were unable to utter a single word; but their eyes told each other all the sentiments of their hearts. Each saw on the other's pale cheek the impress of grief, the trace of tears. Undoubtedly the fresh beauty of the woman one loves is full of charm; but that sickly pallor which comes from separation is far sweeter to the eyes of a lover. A heart of stone melts away under a tearful glance that says without blame, —

"I am happy; I have suffered so much for you and through you."

These few words made the tears spring to Ammalat's eyes. Remembering that he was not alone, he made an effort at self-control, holding up his head; but his voice rebelled, and it was with great difficulty that he succeeded in saying, —

"It is, indeed, a long time since we have seen each other, Sultanetta!"

"And we came very near never seeing each other again, Ammalat," replied Sultanetta. "We were very nearly parted forever."

"Forever!" returned Ammalat, reproachfully. "You could think that, believe that, when there is a world in which beings meet who have loved each other in this one. Oh, had I lost the talisman of my happiness, with what scorn would I have flung away that rag they call life! Oh, I should not have struggled long, no. To have been vanquished would be to have rejoined you."

"Then why do I not die?" said Sultanetta, smiling. "You make out the other world to be so beautiful that it must be better than this, Ammalat, and I should like to go as soon as possible."

"Oh, no, no, Sultanetta; make no such impious wish. You must live a long time for happiness — "

He was about to add, "for love;" he stopped.

Gradually the roses of health budded on the young girl's cheeks. The breath of happiness caused them to bloom.

At the end of eight days things had resumed their ordinary course, and all went as before Ammalat's departure from Khunsack.

Khan Ackmeth made inquiries of Ammalat as to the number and position of the Russian troops.

The khaness questioned him about the fashions and jewels of the women; and as often as Ammalat told her that their women wore neither trousers nor veils, she invoked Allah's holy name.

Assured that health was returning to Sultanetta, Ammalat began to be gloomy. Often, in the midst of a cheerful, happy conversation, he would pause, his head would fall upon his breast, and his eyes fill with tears. Profound sighs seemed to rend his bosom. Sometimes he would spring from his place as if touched by an electric spark. His eyes shot angry flames, and, with a cold smile, he would caress the hilt of his kandjiar. Then, as if yielding to invisible bonds, he would groan, become pensive, and even Sultanetta could not win him from his revery.

Once, at such a time, the lovers being quite alone, Sultanetta, leaning upon his shoulder, said to him, —

"You are sad, my poor heart! you are tired of staying near me!"

"Oh, don't cast such a reproach on one who loves you better than heaven," said Ammalat. "But I have already tried the hell of separation, and I cannot think of it without anguish. Oh, I would a hundred times rather die than leave you again, my beautiful Sultanetta."

"Leave me! you speak of leaving me! If you think of separation, it must be that you desire it."

"Oh, don't poison my wound with suspicion, Sultanetta. Until now you have known but one thing, — how to flourish like a rose, how to fly like a bird. Until now, twice happy child, your wish has been your only guide; but as for me, I am a man. Fate has welded about my neck a chain of steel, and the end of that chain is in the hands of a man, a friend, my benefactor. Duty and gratitude summon me to Derbend"

"A chain! a friend! a benefactor! duty! how many words does it take to conceal your desire to leave me? But, before selling your soul to friendship, had you not given it to love? You had no right to pledge what no longer belonged to you, Ammalat. Oh, forget your Verkovsky, forget your Russian friend and your beautiful ladies of Derbend; forget war, forget glory. I hate bloodshed since I saw your blood flow. What do you lack in our mountains for a free and comfortable life? No one will come here to look for you. My father has many horses and plenty of money, while I — I have a great deal of love. Surely, you are not going away! surely, you will stay with me!"

"No, Sultanetta, I cannot, must not stay. To live and die with you is my one prayer, my one desire; but all that depends on your father. For having listened to Ackmeth Khan I was about to die a death both cruel and infamous. A Russian saved my life. Can I now wed the daughter of the Russians' implacable foe? If your father will let me make his peace with them, Sultanetta, I shall be the happiest of men."

"You know my father," answered Sultanetta, sadly. "Day by day his hatred of the Russians increases, if it were possible. He will sacrifice both of us to his hatred. Besides, fate has decreed that the colonel should kill the noukar whom he had sent for Ibrahim."

"Yes, Sultanetta, like you I regret the death of that man. And yet it was owing to that circumstance that I learned of what was happening here, that I saw you again. If that man were alive, you would be dead."

"Well, try your influence with my father."

"Do you think that it would be my first attempt? Alas! Every time that I have spoken to Ackmeth Khar of my hopes, 'Swear enmity to the Russians,' he has answered, 'and then I will listen to you.'"

"That means that we must renounce hope."

Clasping Sultanetta in his arms, the young man strained her to his heart.

"Why must we say good-bye to hope?" he asked; "are you, then, chained to Avarie?"

"I do not understand you," said the young girl, fixing upon him her limpid and questioning eyes.

"Love me more than all the world, Sultanetta, more than your father, more than your mother, more than your country, and then you will understand me. Sultanetta, I cannot live without you. If you love me, Sultanetta — "

"If I love you!" returned the young girl, proudly.

"Fly from here, Sultanetta; let us leave Khunsack."

"Fly!" repeated she. "Oh, my God! the daughter of the khan to fly like a fugitive, like a guilty thing, like a criminal! It is frightful, unheard of, impossible!"

"Do not tell me that, Sultanetta. If the sacrifice is great, my love is infinite. Order me to die, and I will die with the greatest contempt for life. Do you wish more than my life? Would you have my soul? I will cast it to the lowest depths of hell at a word from you. You are the khan's daughter; but my uncle wears the crown of a principality. And I, too, am a prince, and, I swear it, Sultanetta, worthy of you."

"But my father's revenge, — you forget that, unhappy man!"

"In the course of time, he will himself forget; on seeing how much I love you, and finding that you are happy, he will forgive. His heart is not of stone; our caresses will soften him, our tears melt him, and then, Sultanetta, fortune will cover us with its golden wings.

and then we can proudly say, 'To ourselves we owe our happiness.' "

"My dear love," said Sultanetta, sadly shaking her head, "I have had small experience as yet; but do you know what my heart tells me? That one cannot be happy through ingratitude and deceit. Let us wait, since we cannot do otherwise without sacrificing the happiness of one of us, and we shall see what it will please Allah to send us."

"Allah inspired me with that thought; he will do nothing more for us. Have pity on me, Sultanetta; let us fly, if you do not wish the hour of marriage to sound above my tomb. I have given my word that I would return to Derbend, I must keep my word and keep it promptly. But to go without hope of seeing you again, with the agony of knowing that you will one day be the wife of another, is fearful, insupportable, impossible. If not out of love for me, Sultanetta, then let it be through your pity. Partake of my lot, do not hunt me from my Paradise, do not cause me to lose my reason. You do not know to what point of folly a defrauded passion can carry a heart like mine. I can forget all, trample all under foot, — the sanctity of the fireside, the hospitality of your parents; I can astonish bandits of most renowned fame by the bloody repute of my name. I can make the angels of heaven weep at the sight of my crimes. Sultanetta, save me from the curses of others, save me from your own scorn. Night has fallen, my horses are as swift as the wind; let us fly to kindly Russia, and wait there till the storm is past. For the last time, I implore you, on my knees, with clasped hands. Shame or glory, life or death, all rest on one word from you, — yes or no."

Restrained on the one hand by maidenly fear and her

respect for ancient usages, tempted on the other by the love and fiery eloquence of her lover, Sultanetta drifted uncertainly on that stormy sea whose every wave was a passion; at last she rose, and, wiping away the tears that shone upon her long lashes, with as much pride as resolution, she replied, —

"Ammalat, do not tempt me; love's flame, all shining as it is, does not blind me; I shall always know how to distinguish between right and wrong and good and evil. It is base, Ammalat, to abandon one's family, to repay with ingratitude the long care and infinite tenderness of parents who have reared us. Ah, judge now if I love you, Ammalat! even while knowing the extent of my sacrifice, even while measuring the extent of my crime, — even so, Ammalat, I answer, Yes! and I say, My dear love, I consent to fly with you, for I value you above all the blessings and all the virtues in the world. I am yours, Ammalat. But know this well: it was not your speech that influenced me, but your heart. Allah willed that I should meet and love you; let our hearts then be bound together from this hour on, although the tie which binds us be a withe of thorn! All is at an end, Ammalat; we no longer have but one destiny, one heart, one life, one future. Let us go!"

If the azure curtains of the sky itself had fallen upon Ammalat veiling him from the sun, he could not have been happier than he was at the moment when that consent, so devoted, so complete, so tender, fell from the lips of Sultanetta.

That same hour all was fixed upon for the flight of the two lovers.

The next evening, Ammalat was to depart on a grand hunt which would be supposed to last for three days; but he would return on the same evening. The night was favorable, as there was no moon. Sultanetta was to descend from her window by means of two scarfs knotted one to the other: Ammalat would receive her in his arms.

Horses would be awaiting them in the little chapel where Sultanetta and Ammalat had met after the tiger-hunt.

And then, woe to the enemy in the path who should try to bar their way!

A kiss sealed the compact, and they separated full of joy and fear.

The longed-for morrow came. Ammalat visited his horse, prepared his arms, and passed the entire day in consulting the sun.

One would have said that he, too, the star with golden rays, hesitated in his course, unwilling to leave that brilliant, warm sky and sink into the snows of the Caucasus.

Ammalat waited for the night as for his affianced.

Oh, how slowly moved that sun! how the heavenly traveller loitered along his luminous path, what a wide gulf still remained between hope and happiness!

Four o'clock in the afternoon sounded: it is the Mussulman's dinner hour. They were grouped around the rug; but Ackmeth Khan was very sad.

His eyes flashed under his knitted brows. Often they rested now on his daughter and now on his guest. Sometimes the lines of his face would contract into a derisive look. But that expression would soon be lost in the paleness of anger. His remarks were scoffing and brief, and all caused repentance to spring up in the heart of Sultanetta and fear in the mind of Ammalat.

Sultanetta's mother, as if she could have foreseen the threatened separation, was tenderer and more thoughtful than usual, and Sultanetta more than once came near bursting into tears and throwing herself into her mother's arms.

After dinner, Khan Ackmeth called Ammalat into the court. The horses were already saddled for the chase. Four noukars whom Ammalat had sent for were in waiting, mingling with the noukars of the khan.

"Let us try my new falcon," said the khan to Ammalat. "The evening is fine, it is not too warm, and we can still between now and night get a few pheasants or partridges."

Ammalat could not but comply; he nodded assent and sprang on his horse.

Ackmeth Khan and the young beg proceeded side by side, — Ammalat pensive, Khan Ackmeth silent. On the left and along a rocky steep, a mountaineer was climbing. His feet were equipped with iron crampoons by means of which he clung to the rocky crags, with the further aid of an iron claw at the extremity of his staff.

A hat full of wheat was fastened in front of him, at his belt.

A long Tartar musket was slung across his shoulders.

Khan Ackmeth halted and, pointing him out to Ammalat, said, —

"Look at that old man; at the risk of his life, he is hunting among the rocks for a little patch of earth in which to sow some grain. He harvests it with bleeding toil, and often it is only at the price of his blood that he defends his flock against men and wild beasts. His country is poverty-stricken. Ah, well, ask him, Ammalat, why he loves his country so much, why he does not change it for a richer land. He will answer: 'Here I am free; here I owe no man tribute; these snows guard my pride and my independence.' That independence the Russians would take from him, and you yourself, Ammalat, have become the Russians' slave."

"Khan," answered the young man, lifting his head, "you know very well that I have been overcome, not by the power of the Russians, but by their good-will. I am not their slave, I am their friend."

"Well, it is the greater shame to you, then; the chamkal's heir casts about for golden fetters! Ammalat Beg lives at the expense of Colonel Verkovsky!"

"Don't say that, Khan Ackmeth. Verkovsky, before giving me bread and salt, gave me life. He loves me, I love him. Let that be said once for all, and let us say no more about it."

"There is no such thing as a friendship with unbelievers. To fight when we meet, to exterminate them when we can, these are the laws of the Koran and the duty of a true follower of the Prophet."

"Khan, don't meddle with the bones of the Prophet; you are no mullah to tell me my duty. I know what I have to do as a man of honor, and I shall do it. I have within me the sense of right and of wrong. Let us talk of something else."

"This sense, Ammalat, should be in your heart rathe than on your lips."

Ammalat gave a sign of impatience.

But, taking no notice of this sign, which he had per fectly understood, Khan Ackmeth proceeded: —

"A last time, Ammalat, will you listen to the coun sels of a friend? Will you abandon the unbelievers and stay with us?"

"I would have given my life for the happiness you hold out to me, Khan Ackmeth," said the young man, with a tone of conviction which there was no mistaking;

"but I have sworn to return to Derbend, and I shall keep my oath."

"That is your final decision?"

"It is final."

"Then, Ammalat, your oath must be the more quickly fulfilled. I have known you a long time, you know me also. We must not even attempt to deceive each other. I will not conceal from you that I had cherished the hope of calling you my son. I rejoiced that you loved Sultanetta. Your captivity weighed on my heart, your long absence was one of the sorrows of my life. At last you have returned to the house of the khan, and you have found everything as before your departure. But you have not brought us your heart again. It is sad; but what can be done? Ammalat, I would never accept a slave of the Russians for a son-in-law!"

"Ackmeth Khan!"

"Oh, let me conclude. Your unexpected arrival, your grief in Sultanetta's room, your exclamations, your sobs, your despair, exposed to all the world your love and our intentions. Throughout all Avarie you are known as my daughter's betrothed; but, now that the tie binding us is broken, we must cut short all these suppositions; for the sake of Sultanetta's peace of mind, for her reputation, you must leave us at once. Ammalat, we part still friends, but we shall meet only as kinsmen. May Allah in his goodness change your heart, and permit us to see you again as an inseparable friend. That is my dearest wish, my most earnest prayer; but until then, adieu!"

And, turning his horse face about, without adding a word Ackmeth Khan set off at full speed.

A thunderbolt, striking at Ammalat's feet and opening an abyss, could not have overcome him more than did these last words from Ackmeth Khan. Motionless, thunderstruck, he stood rooted to the spot, breathlessly watching horse and rider, who already seemed but a cloud of dust.

An hour later he was still on the same spot; but by that time night had fallen.

The night was dark.

XII.

In order to arrest the revolt of Daghestan, Colonel Verkovsky was with his regiment in the village of Kjaffir Koumieck.

The tent of Ammalat Beg was pitched beside that of the colonel.

Sophyr Ali, the young foster-brother of Ammalat, who appeared in the beginning of this story, was lying within the tent and drinking by the glassful that foaming wine called the champagne of the Don.

Colonel Verkovsky had sent for the young man to come from Tarki, hoping that the sight of him, together with his friendship, would distract Ammalat Beg from his melancholy.

In fact, Ammalat Beg was more than melancholy, he was wrapped in gloom.

Haggard, pale, brooding, he kept within the seclusion of his tent, lying on his cushions and smoking.

Three months previously, driven, like the first sinner, from Paradise, he had come to rejoin the colonel and was camping with his regiment.

In sight of the mountains whither his heart took wing but where his feet were forbidden, he preyed upon himself; anger flared up in his soul, like a half-extinguished light, at the first word. Rancor, like a slow sure poison, spread more and more in his veins. Bitterness was on his lips, hatred in his eyes.

"In faith," said Sophyr Ali, "wine is a good thing! Since we are forbidden to drink it, it must be that Mahomet got hold of some bad wine. Really, these drops are so sweet one can believe that an angel's tears fell into the bottle. Take a glass and drink, Ammalat. Your heart will rise on the wine as light as a cork. You know what Hafiz, the Persian poet, says about it."

"I know that you bore me to death, Sophyr Ali. Then let me hire you to spare me this nonsense, charge it up to Saadi even, as well as Hafiz."

"Ammalat, Ammalat, you are very hard on your poor Sophyr Ali. What would come of it if he were as hard on you? Doesn't he listen patiently when you talk to him of Sultanetta? Love makes you mad; with me it is wine. But my madness has lucid intervals, the occasions when I am not drunk, while you have none; you are ever in love. To the health of Sultanetta!"

"I have already told you that I forbid your uttering her name, especially when you are drunk."

"Then here's to the health of the Russians!"

Ammalat shrugged his shoulders.

"Well!" said Sophyr Ali, who was getting more and more tipsy, "you will be forbidding me to drink the health of the Russians next!"

"What have the Russians done for you that you should love them so much?"

"What have they done to you that you should hate them?"

"They have done nothing to me, but I have observed them close at hand. They are no better than we Tartars. They are covetous, back-biting, idle. How long a time have they been masters here, and in all the time of their mastership what good have they done, what laws have they introduced, what learning have they spread abroad? Verkovsky has opened my eyes to the bad side of my fellow-countrymen, and at the same time I have seen the faults of his; and their defects are the more unpardonable in them because they have grown up surrounded by good examples. But these good examples they forget here for the sake of applying themselves only to the unclean appetites of the body."

"Ammalat, Ammalat, I should hope that you would except Verkovsky at least."

"Of course, he is the exception, he and a few others; but, in your opinion, even, are there many of whom we can say as much?"

"Are not the angels of heaven to be counted too? No, no, look at it: Verkovsky is a marvel of goodness. You will not even find a Tartar who speaks ill of him. Every soldier would give his soul for him. — Abdul Amid, more wine! — To the health of Verkovsky, Ammalat!"

"Just now I would not drink the health of Mahomet, even."

"Why, if your heart were not as black as the eyes of your Sultanetta, you would drink Verkovsky's health. Ammalat, were this to reach the beard of the mufti of Derbend, every imam and all the prophets would be up in arms against you!"

"Let me alone."

"It is not right, Ammalat. I would raise the devil with my own blood for you, and you, you, — out upon you! you refuse to take a drop of wine with me."

"No, Sophyr Ali, I will not take it, and I will not take it, because I do not want it; and I do not want it, do you hear? because my blood is already too hot as it is."

"A mere excuse, and a poor excuse at that! It is not our first drink, is it? Not the first time our blood has boiled? Wonderful stuff, Asiatic blood! Speak out, be frank, you have a grudge against the colonel?"

"Well, yes, I have."

" And can one know why ? "

" Why ? "

" Yes."

" For many reasons."

" But one ? "

" For some time now he has been pouring poison into the honey of his friendship. Now, the poison that he has let fall drop by drop, drop by drop, has filled the cup; and behold the cup is running over. I hate friends that are too solicitous; they are good for advice, — that is, for what involves them in neither trouble nor risk."

" I see; he did not let you return to Avarie, and you cannot forgive him for refusing."

" If you had my heart in your breast, Sophyr Ali, you would understand the cruelty of such a refusal. Ackmeth Khan has softened, it seems: he asks to see me, and I cannot go to him. Oh! Sultanetta! Sultanetta! " cried the young man, wringing his hands in his anger.

" For my part, I say, put yourself in Verkovsky's place, and tell me frankly whether you would not have done as he is doing."

" No. From the beginning, I should have said: 'Ammalat, do not count on me; Ammalat, do not ask me to help you in anything.' I do not desire his help, only that he should not hinder me. No, he stands between me and the sun of my happiness. He does it out of friendship, he says; he asks me to let him direct my life, — he gives me poppy-juice to put me to sleep! "

" What matters the remedy, Ammalat, provided that it cures you ? "

" And who asks him to cure me, pray ? The divine malady of love, the only one of which one could wish to die, is my sole happiness, my only joy. If he takes that from me, my heart will follow."

When Ammalat finished speaking, night had already fallen, and yet he could see that the presence of a stranger at the door of his tent was rendering the darkness more obscure.

"Who is there?" demanded Ammalat.

"Is any one bringing my wine?" said Sophyr Ali. "My bottle is empty."

The shadow drew near without any response.

"Who is there?" repeated Ammalat, laying his hand on his kandjiar.

A name uttered in a tone so low that it was breathed in his ear like a sigh, caused Ammalat Beg to tremble:

"Nephtali!"

At the same time the shadow withdrew and left the tent.

Ammalat Beg bounded to his feet, and followed the form scarcely visible through the darkness.

Sophyr Ali followed Ammalat.

The night was gloomy, the fires were out, the line of sentinels was at a distance.

Finally, the form halted.

"Is it really you, Nephtali?" asked Ammalat.

"Speak low, Ammalat," answered the other; "I am not a friend of the Russians myself."

"Ah!" said Ammalat, "you too, you have come here to reproach me? I should have thought you had a kinder mission for your brother."

He extended his hand.

Nephtali took Ammalat's hand and pressed it convulsively.

In the young mountaineer's friendship for Ammalat, was something which the latter could not explain; one would have said that the Tchetchen was constrained to do violence to himself in order to love Ammalat.

SULTANETTA. 149

"Speak," insisted Ammalat; "what news do you bring? How is Ackmeth Khan? Is Sultanetta well?"

"Ammalat," said Nephtali, "I am not sent to answer your questions, but to question you. Will you follow me?"

"Where?"

"Where I am charged to conduct you."

"What shall I do there?"

"You know from whom I come?"

"No."

"'The eagle loves the mountain.'"

Ammalat recognized Ackmeth Khan's favorite saying.

"You come from the khan?" said he.

"Will you follow me, Ammalat?"

"How far?"

"Four versts from here."

"Must we go on foot?"

"Are you at liberty to leave the camp on horseback?"

"Yes. But, that I may not arouse suspicion, I must notify the colonel."

"That is, you can go the length of your chain, but not leave it. Notify the colonel."

"Sophyr Ali, tell the colonel that we are going, for diversion, on a jaunt into the country. Get my gun and saddle my horse."

Sophyr Ali sighed; but, as his bottle was empty, it was the less difficult to obey. In a little while they heard the step of two horses.

It was Sophyr Ali riding one horse, and leading Ammalat's.

"Here," said he, "take your gun; I have renewed the priming. It is in good condition; you can rest easy."

"And why do you come?"

"Because the colonel asked me if I was going, and I

told him yes, and now if they saw you leaving without me it would look suspicious."

Ammalat comprehended the young man's motive: he had not meant to leave him alone in the dark with a stranger.

Nephtali was unknown to Sophyr Ali, although Sophyr Ali had heard his name.

"Can he come with us?" asked Ammalat of Nephtali.

"Yes, and no."

"Explain yourself."

"Yes, as far as to the entrance of the camp; no, to the rendezvous."

"Come," said Ammalat to Sophyr Ali.

And he sprang on his horse.

"And you?" demanded he of Nephtali.

"Don't worry about me, Ammalat; I came into camp without you, and I am very well able to leave it without you."

"Where shall I find you again?"

"It is not for you to find me; it is for me to find you."

And Nephtali was lost in the darkness, making no more noise than a ghost.

Ammalat and Sophyr Ali headed for the first sentinel, gave the password and went on.

Every evening, the password was communicated to Ammalat by Colonel Verkovsky. It was a delicate attention from the latter, although Ammalat well understood that he was only a prisoner on parole.

Twenty paces beyond the sentinel, Ammalat trembled in spite of himself. A third horseman was advancing beside them. He had arisen without any one's knowing whence he came. He might have issued from the ground.

"Ha!" ejaculated Sophyr Ali; "who goes there?"

"Silence!" said Nephtali.

"Silence!" repeated Ammalat Beg.

Sophyr Ali held his tongue, but not without muttering; the second bottle, abandoned just as it was about to be brought, stuck in his crop. At every step he grew angry, at the darkness, at the bushes, at the ditches. He coughed, spat, swore, in the hope of making one or the other of his companions say something; but it was useless: both remained dumb.

Finally, after a pause, his horse stumbled against a stone.

"The devil take our guide, who, for that matter, looks very much as if he had come in his own interests! Who knows where he is taking us? He is capable of leading us into some trap."

"There is no danger," answered Ammalat; "he is a messenger from a friend and is himself my friend."

"Oh! yes, that is quite possible; you have made many new friends since we took leave of each other, Ammalat. — May the new be as devoted to you as the old!"

They had left the main road and had plunged into a sort of undergrowth of those shrubs with the obstinate thorns, known to every traveller in the Caucasus.

"In the name of the king of Spirits," said Sophyr Ali to his guide, "tell us quickly whether you are in league with these bushes to get the galloon off my tchouska. Don't you know a better road? I am neither a snake nor a fox."

Nephtali halted.

"You are in luck," said he. "Your journey is ended; stay here and hold the horses."

"And Ammalat?" said Sophyr Ali.

"Ammalat goes with me."

"Where?"

"To mind his own business, apparently."

"Ammalat," cried Sophyr Ali, "will you go without me into the mountain with this bandit?"

"Which means," replied Ammalat, dismounting, "that you do not care to remain alone."

He tossed the bridle over the other's arm.

"As for that," said Sophyr Ali, "I would a hundred times rather be alone here than in the company of the knave that came for you."

"You will not be alone," said Ammalat Beg, smiling; "I leave you in delightful company, that of the wolves and jackals. There, do you hear them singing? Listen!"

"God trust that I shall not have to get your bones away from those songsters to-morrow morning," said Sophyr Ali.

They separated.

As he went away Ammalat heard Sophyr Ali loading his gun by way of precaution at all events.

Nephtali led Ammalat through the thicket as readily as if it had been broad daylight. One would have thought the young Tchetchen possessed the power, accorded by nature to certain animals, of seeing as well by night as by day.

After a demi-verst through bushes and over stones, the road began to descend; finally, after a very difficult passage the road became a little better, and they reached the entrance of a recess, in the depths of which a brushwood fire was burning.

Ackmeth Khan was reclining beside the fire, his gun across his knees.

At the noise made by the two young men, he raised himself upon his bourka.

By the quickness of the movement, it was easy to see that he waited impatiently.

Recognizing Ammalat, he stood up.

Ammalat cast himself upon his neck.

"I am glad to see you, Ammalat," said the khan, "and I am weak enough not to conceal the feeling from you. But I hasten to say that it is not for a simple interview that I have put you to this inconvenience. Be seated, Ammalat, and let us talk of a serious matter."

"For me, khan?"

"For both of us. I was your father's friend, and there was a time when I was yours."

"Is the time gone by, then?"

"No. It depended on you that it should last forever. You did not desire it; or rather, no, it was not you who did not desire it."

"Who, then?"

"That demon of a Verkovsky."

"Khan, you do not know him."

"You are the one who do not know him, but you very soon will, I hope. Meanwhile let us speak of Sultanetta."

Ammalat's heart gave a bound.

"You know that I desired to make her your wife, Ammalat; you refused the conditions on which I could give her to you. We will talk no more of that; I presume that you reflected as a man must do on serious occasions in life. But you will understand one thing: she cannot, and moreover must not, remain unmarried. It would be a dishonor to my house."

Ammalat felt the perspiration beading his forehead.

"Ammalat," continued Ackmeth Khan, "her hand has been demanded."

Ammalat felt his knees give way; the heart in his breast almost ceased to beat.

Finally his voice returned.

"And who is this bold wooer?" he demanded.

"The second son of Chamkal Abdul Moussaline. After you he is certainly, of all the mountain princes, the most worthy to become the husband of Sultanetta."

"After me?" said Ammalat. "But, by Mahomet, it strikes me that you talk as if I were dead; has my memory then quite died out of the hearts of my friends?"

"No, Ammalat, your memory has not died out of my heart, and just now I confessed to you yourself that I was glad to see you; but be as frank as I am sincere; I leave you to judge your own cause; what more do you wish? What more do you exact? What must we do, what can we do? You will not leave the Russians; I myself cannot become their friend."

"Yes, it is possible. You have only to desire, only to say the word, and all will be forgotten, all will be overlooked. I will wager my head upon it, and can answer on the word of Verkovsky; it would be the best thing for you, for the peace of the Avares, for Sultanetta's happiness, for mine. Oh! I beg of you, I beseech you, I implore you on my knees, on my knees! Ackmeth Khan, be the friend of the Russians, and everything, even your rank, will be restored to you."

"You answer for the lives of others, you who are not even the master of your own liberty!"

"Who wants my life, who frets about my liberty, when I spurn them myself?"

"Who wants your life, child that you are? Do you think that the pillow under Chamkal Tarkovsky's head does not turn of itself when he thinks of you as the heir to his principality of Tarki, and that you are the friend of the Russians?"

"I have never sought his friendship, I have never feared him as an enemy."

" Fear not, but despise not, Ammalat. Do you know that an envoy has been sent to Yermolof to tell him to kill you for a traitor? Formerly, he would have killed you with a kiss, if it had been possible; but now that you have sent back his daughter, your father-in-law no longer hides his wrath, and he will use ball or poniard."

" Under Verkovsky's protection, no one can reach me, except an assassin. From assassins, Allah save me!"

" Listen, Ammalat, I will tell you a fable. A sheep, pursued by wolves, fled into a kitchen. He found shelter there, was well lodged, well fed; he loudly boasted of the care that was taken of him, and he had never been so happy.

" Three days later, he was roasted!

" Ammalat, that is your story.

" It is time that I open your eyes. The man whom you call the first among your friends has betrayed you first. You are surrounded by traitors, Ammalat. My principal desire in summoning you to an interview was to forewarn you. When Sultanetta's hand was asked, I was given to understand, on behalf of the chamkal, that through him I could become a friend of the Russians much more safely than through Ammalat, who was now an object of distrust even with those who are answerable for him. Besides, those who are answerable for you will very soon be rid of you. They will put you out of the way where you are no longer to be feared. I have suspected much, and have learned more than I suspected. To-day, I stopped a noukar of the chamkal's; he was sent to Verkovsky, under some pretext of which I know nothing, about which I am not concerned. What does trouble me is that the chamkal gives six thousand roubles to the one who will kill you. Verkovsky is not concerned in that, of course; but, master of the chamkal, he is not the master of his government. You are guilty of treason. After swearing fealty to the Russians, you have been taken in arms. They spare your life, perhaps; but something, indeed, must be done with you. You are to be sent to Siberia."

"I?" cried Ammalat.

"Listen, and see if I am not well informed. To-morrow the regiment returns to its quarters; to-morrow a meeting, at which you and your fate will be discussed at great length, will be held in your own house at Bouinaky. They will prepare denunciations against you and get together a certain number of complaints. They will poison you with your own bread, Ammalat, and fasten an iron chain around your neck while promising you mountains of gold."

If Ackmeth Khan desired to see Ammalat suffer, he had that sorry pleasure during all the time that he was talking. Every word, like a sharpened red-hot iron, stabbed the young beg's heart; all his beliefs were destroyed, if the half of what the khan said was true. He repeatedly endeavored to interrupt him, to answer him; each time the words died on his lips. The wild beast that, tamed by Verkovsky, lay sleeping within Ammalat, gradually became aroused by the words of Ackmeth Khan; already it shook its chain, a little more and the chain would break.

At last a torrent of threats and curses escaped from the young man's mouth.

"Ah! if you are not lying," cried he, "ah! if you are telling the truth, Ackmeth Khan, woe to them that have abused my good faith and taken advantage of my gratitude! Let me have proof of what you say, and then revenge, revenge!"

"That is the first word worthy of you that has left your mouth, Ammalat," said Khan Ackmeth, not even attempting to conceal his joy at the wrath of the young prince.. "You have bowed your head too long at the feet of the Russians. It is time for the eagle to spread his wings and fly above the clouds. You will have a better view of your enemies from up there. Give them vengeance for vengeance, death for death!"

"Oh! yes!" replied Ammalat; "death to the chamkal who bargains for my life! Death to Abdul Moussaline, who puts out his hand for my treasure!"

"Yes, death to them, by all means! but do not lose sight of another enemy whom you are omitting from your vengeance, and who threatens your destiny in quite another way from either of those whom you have just named."

A chill ran through Ammalat's veins.

"You mean Verkovsky?" said he, drawing back in spite of himself. "You are wrong, Khan Ackmeth; he cannot desire my death who saved me from death, — and such a death! an infamous death!"

"To give you over to an infamous life, Ammalat. And, for that matter, have you not saved his life too, — once from the attacks of a wild boar, again, from a Lesghian's poniard? Balance your accounts properly, Ammalat, and Verkovsky is the one in debt."

"No, no, Ackmeth Khan," said the young man, violently striking his breast with his hand; "no! a voice speaking louder than yours tells me that I am not at quits with Verkovsky; it is the voice of conscience."

Ackmeth Khan shrugged his shoulders.

"Conscience! conscience!" muttered he. "Come, Ammalat, I see clearly that without me you will not know how to set about anything, not even to marry Sultanetta. Then. listen: —

"Of the one who wishes to become my son-in-law, the first, the last, the only thing I ask, in exchange for which he will secure the hand of Sultanetta, is the life of Verkovsky. Verkovsky is the head of Daghestan. Let that head fall and the whole of Daghestan is decapitated. I have two thousand men ready to rise at a word from me. With them, I can descend like an avalanche upon Tarki; and supposing that you should be the one to merit Sultanetta's hand, it would make you not only the chamkal of Tarki, but of the whole of Daghestan as well. Your fate is in your own hands as it has never been in another man's. Choose: either a prison — eternal exile in Siberia, at least — or happiness with Sultanetta, power with me. After all, perhaps I have judged you ill and you have neither ambition nor love in your heart. And now, farewell! but remember that the first, the only time that we meet again, it will be as devoted kinsmen or as mortal enemies."

And Ackmeth Khan disappeared before Ammalat had time to think of detaining him.

He remained a long time motionless and silent, with his head drooped over his breast. Finally, he raised himself, looked about, and saw Nephtali waiting for him.

Without a word, the young Tchetchen led him to where Sophyr Ali was awaiting him with the two horses. Ammalat silently extended a hand to him in token of thanks, and left him without even pronouncing the name of Sultanetta.

Then, silent still, he mounted his horse, regained the camp, entered his tent, and flung himself upon his couch.

Then only did he turn and writhe with stifled cries and moans.

All the serpents of hell were let loose in his heart.

XIII.

"Son of a she-wolf, will you be still?" an old woman was saying to her grandson, awakened and crying before day. "Be still, or I will send you out in the street to sleep."

The old Tartar woman had been Ammalat's nurse. Her house was built near the beg's palace. It was a present from her foster-child.

We caught a glimpse of her in the first chapter of this story, watching the prowess of Ammalat Beg.

This house to which we are conducting our readers, one-storied and surmounted by a terrace like all Tartar houses, consisted of two rooms neatly arranged. The floor was carpeted. The corners were occupied by chests, bright with decorations of ironwork, on which were rolled up some feather beds with their blankets, symbols of competence in Tartar homes. On shelves suspended against the wall was an array of tin-plated pilaff-cups shining like silver. The old woman's face was stamped with the constant bad-humor which is the bitter fruit of a sad and solitary life, and, like the worthy representative of her compatriots that she was, she never ceased to scold and grumble at her grandson, at the top of her voice and from morning till night.

"Keep still, Kesse!" she cried again, "or I will hand you over to five hundred thousand devils! Don't you hear the noise they make on the roof, and how they are scratching on the window-panes to get at you?"

The night was dark, the rain was falling in torrents. The storm beat on the terrace and against the windows, and the wind swirling through the chimney sounded like wailing sobs accompanying nature's tears.

The little boy stopped crying, and, opening his great eyes with their black lashes, he listened fearfully to the divers noises of the tempest.

But a noise more terrifying began to mingle with this uproar, and in spite of the advanced hour of the night — it was almost three o'clock in the morning — there was a knocking at the door.

And then it was the old woman's turn to be frightened.

Her bosom friend, an old black dog, lifted his head and plaintively howled.

The knocking was redoubled, and, in tones of distinguishable anger, an unknown voice cried, —

"Atch Kaninii! Akhirine! Akhirisi! Will you ever open the door?"

"*Allah bismillah!*" exclaimed the old woman, first looking at the ceiling, then kicking her dog, then trying to calm the little boy, who had begun to cry again. "Who is there? Who can be knocking at this hour? What well-meaning man would come on such a night and knock at a poor old woman's door? Are you the devil? Then go to neighbor Kachtkina's. It is time to show her the road to hell. But if you are not the devil in person, be off! My son is not at home, if you happen to have business with him. He is with Ammalat Beg. As for me, the beg has retired me; and so you cannot be coming from him. I owe him neither ducks, nor hens, nor eggs; he has freed me from all rent. *Dame!* You may be sure that I did not bring him up for nothing."

"You besom of hell, will you open the door for me?" cried the impatient voice; "if not, I will splinter your door so that not a board shall be left to make you a coffin."

"You are welcome, you are welcome," said the old woman, hastening to the door and opening it with trembling hand.

The door swung on its hinges, and a man short of stature, but with a handsome yet gloomy countenance, appeared on the threshold.

He wore the Circassian costume. The water streamed from his bachlik and his white bourka. He threw the latter on the woman's bed without ceremony, and began to unfasten the bachlik which concealed his face. Fatma, in the meantime, lighted her candle and stood before the new-comer, trembling in every joint. The dog, taking his tail between his legs, thrust himself into a corner; and the little boy betook himself to the fireplace, which, never having a fire in it, was rather an ornament than a useful piece of architecture.

"Well, Fatma," said the new-comer, when he had finished taking off his bachlik, "you have grown proud, it seems; you do not recognize an old friend?"

Fatma regarded the stranger curiously, and an expression of relief overspread her face.

She recognized Ackmeth Khan, who, during this stormy night, had come from Kjaffir Koumieck to Bouinaky.

"May the sand blind my wicked eyes for not having known their old master!" said the crone, crossing her hands on her breast in token of submission and respect. "To tell the truth, khan, they are put out by the tears that I have shed for my country, — for poor Avarie. Forgive the unhappy Fatma, khan; she is old, and old age does not see much at night besides the grave that death is digging for it."

"Come, come, you are not so old as you make out.

Fatma. I remember, child, to have seen you as a young girl at Khunsack."

"The strange country ages the stranger," responded Fatma. "In our mountains, khan, I should still perhaps be fruit worth culling; but here I am a wretched handful of snow flung from the mountain into the mud of these streets. Sit here, khan; sit on this cushion, you will be more comfortable. But how can I regale my dear guest? Does the khan need anything?"

"The khan desires you to regale him with your goodwill, that is all."

"I am in your power, khan, you know it well. Command, then, give your orders; it is for your servant to obey."

"Listen, Fatma, I have no time to waste in talk. In few words, this is why I am here: Do me a service with your tongue, and I will rejoice your teeth. I will give you ten sheep if you do what I tell you, and I will clothe you in silk from head to foot, slippers included."

"Ten sheep and a silken gown! Oh, my good chief! oh, my dear khan! Never has such a guest entered my house since I was captured by those cursed Tartars, and was married here against my will. For a silken robe and ten sheep, you can do what you will, you may even cut off one of my ears."

"It is not necessary to cut off your ears, woman; no, it is better that you should use them. This is what I wish: Ammalat will visit you to-day with the colonel. Do you know the colonel?"

"Allah! I should think so, — our mortal enemy."

"That he is! Chamkal Tarkovsky will be with them. The colonel is Ammalat's friend. He is making him drink wine and eat pig!"

SULTANETTA.

"The child that sucked my milk?" cried the old mountain woman with horror.

"Yes. If we are not on guard, before three days Ammalat will be a Christian."

"Mahomet save him!" exclaimed the old woman, as she spat and threw up her hands.

"To save Ammalat from everlasting damnation, you see, woman, we must embroil him with his Verkovsky."

"Am I to take a hand in that, khan? As true as that I am your servant and Allah's, I will do it."

"Yes, pay attention."

"I am not losing a syllable, khan."

The old woman's eyes glittered with fanaticism.

"You are to throw yourself at his feet, to weep as if at the funeral of your own son. You will not need to borrow tears from your neighbors; you love Ammalat well enough to weep for the loss of his soul. You will tell him that you have overheard a conversation between the colonel and the chamkal; that the latter complained of Ammalat's having sent back his daughter; that he said he hated him because of his principality of Tarkovsky, in connection with which Ammalat believed himself to have some rights. You will say that the chamkal begged the colonel to permit him to take Ammalat's life."

"And I shall add that the colonel consented?"

"No, old woman," quickly returned the khan; "he would not believe you. Say, on the contrary, that the colonel was indignant and had answered— Listen now; understand me well."

"I am listening, and I shall understand; never fear."

"And say that the colonel answered: 'All that I can possibly do for you, chamkal — and that only on condition that you will faithfully serve the Russians — is to send him to Siberia.'"

"To Siberia!"

"Come now, repeat what I have said."

The old woman had a good memory, and repeated it word for word. But, for the greater security, the khan required her to repeat it a second time.

"Now," pursued the khan, "embroider that as much as you like. You are celebrated for your tales. But don't get your mouth full of mud now, speak clearly, and add as proof of what you advance that the colonel means to take him to Georgievsk, to get him away from his family and his noukars, and then, to send him in chains to the devil."

Ackmeth added to this falsehood all sorts of details which Fatma stored in her mind, making the khan renew his promise of the ten sheep, and especially of the gown of silk.

The khan pledged himself, and to bind the bargain he gave her a gold piece, a thing so rare among the mountaineers that they make them into ornaments of dress.

"Allah!" cried the old woman, clutching the piece of money in her hand. "May my salt turn to ashes, may I die of hunger, may — "

"Come," interrupted Ackmeth, "enough; don't feed the devil with your oaths; use words to some purpose. Ammalat has great faith in you, I know. Don't forget that his happiness is at stake; that in rescuing him from the Russians, you are extricating him from the hands of the devil. Once convinced that they intend to send him to Siberia, he will leave his new friends and marry my daughter. Then you will all come to live with me in Khunsack, in your old country, and you will end your life singing in the land where you began to sing. But beware! if you betray us, or if you spoil the affair with your prating, I swear, for my part, I, who do not take oaths, to feed the devil on chislik that I have made from your old skin."

"You can be easy, khan; I am an honest woman, to whose flesh the devil has no right. I will keep the secret as securely as if it were in the tomb of my dead, and I will put my shirt on Ammalat."[1]

"Enough, then; and, that the question may not arise at an inopportune moment, I think I must seal your lips with gold."

And the khan drew out a second piece of gold, which he handed to Fatma.

"By my head and my eyes, I am yours!" cried the old woman, seizing and kissing the khan's hand.

Then she fell on her knees to kiss his feet.

Ackmeth Khan drew away in scorn.

"Slavery, slavery," muttered he, "be you accursed, that, for two pieces of gold, can make a human being crawl like a snake!"

And he went away.

---

[1] A Tartar saying: To put one's shirt on another, is to cause him to entertain no opinions except those of the one whose shirt he wears.

XIV.

Colonel Verkovsky to his *fiancée*: —

August, 1822.
In Camp, near the village of Kjaffir Koumieck.

Yes, Ammalat is in love, dear Marie. But how does he love, the lunatic? Never, in my maddest youth, did my love for you — the love that has been my life, moreover! — reach such a length. I myself was scorched like paper ignited by the sun's rays; while he burns like a ship struck by lightning and lost at sea.

Marie, do you remember when we once read — happy time! — Shakspere's "Othello?" Well, "Othello" alone can give you an idea of the tropical flame that leaps through the veins of our Tartar. True, in Ammalat the Tartar is grafted on the Persian.

Now that the ice is broken, he loves to talk long and often of his Sultanetta. And I like to see him blaze up as he talks of her. Sometimes he resembles a cataract falling from the height of a rock, and again he is like one of those naphtha springs of Baku. Like them, he burns with an inextinguishable flame, his cheeks glow, his eyes emit sparks. He is magnificent at such times. I myself am so affected that I open my arms and take him to my bosom, quite broken down by his excitement. Very soon he becomes ashamed of himself. He dares not look at me, releases my hand and goes away; and he spends entire days, after one of these exhibitions, silent and taciturn.

Since his return from Khunsack, he is gloomier than ever, and especially during these last few days.

He has begged me to let him go again to Khunsack to see his love just once more. But I have refused his request. I must guard his honor. With that violent passion, he might fail to keep his word some day, and I should lose the ideal that I have formed of this handsome, noble-hearted young man.

I have written all this to Yermolof. He has told me to take him with me to Georgievsk, where he himself will be. There, through Ammalat, he will form a treaty with Ackmeth Khan, which will be of the greatest utility to Russia, and which may achieve Ammalat's happiness by leading to his union with Sultanetta. I shall be very happy, dear Marie, on the day when I shall make this young man happy! And he, who can never feel by halves, what gratitude he will declare! Then, dear Marie, I will make him get on his knees before you, and I will say: "Adore her; if I had not loved Marie, you would not be the husband of Sultanetta."

Yesterday I received a letter from the lieutenant-governor. How kind he is! He has anticipated all my wishes. Everything is arranged, my love, and I am to join you at the springs. I have only to take my regiment to Derbend, and set off. I shall know neither fatigue by day, nor sleep by night before the hour when I shall rest in your arms. What eagle will lend me his wings for my journey? What giant will lend me his strength to support my happiness? In truth, my heart is so light that to prevent its flying away, I seize my breast with both hands. Could I but sleep until the moment of seeing you again, and until then live only in dreams in which you are present! And yet, my dear love, I awoke this morning as sad as death. I know not what presentiment of evil assails my heart. I left my tent and entered Ammalat's. He was still asleep; his face was pale and haggard. In his heart some hate is struggling with his love. He bears me ill-will for my refusal; but what revenge I shall enjoy on the day when I shall have secured his happiness, when I can say: "Life, what is it? It is Sultanetta, now!"

To-day I shall say good-bye to my mountains of Daghestan for a long time. Who knows? perhaps forever. It is curious, my dear love, when I catch myself gazing at the mountains, sea and sky, by what sweet sadness my heart is both oppressed and expanded.

O my dear soul! how happy I am that I can now say with assurance: Till we meet again!

XV.

THE poison of the lie seared Ammalat's heart and spread through his veins.

His nurse Fatma had conscientiously earned her ten sheep, her silk gown, and her two pieces of gold.

She had on that very evening plied him at length with all the khan's conspiracy, Ammalat having come to Bouinaky with the colonel, and the colonel having had an interview with the chamkal.

He had tried at first to doubt; but how could he suspect Fatma, his good nurse, who loved him like a son, to be the accomplice of Ackmeth Khan?

The poisoned arrow had lodged deep in his heart. In his first transport of rage, he wished to kill both the colonel and the chamkal.

His veneration for the dues of hospitality withheld him.

He postponed his revenge till a later time, but as one puts his dagger into its sheath, only to draw it forth keen and deadly.

Thus the day went by; the regiment halted for two hours' rest.

During these two hours, this is what Ammalat wrote to Ackmeth Khan, hoping to relieve his heart by unburdening it on paper: —

"Midnight.

"Ackmeth Khan! Ackmeth Khan! why have you flashed this light into my eyes? Do you know that its flame has entered my breast? Oh! friendship forgotten! a brother betrayed! a brother murdered! what terrible extremes, and between them but a step, — or an abyss!

"I cannot sleep, I can think of nothing else. I am chained to this thought, like a prisoner to the wall of his dungeon. A sea of blood flows in upon me, and lightnings flash above the dark waves, instead of stars.

"My soul is like a rock to which the wild birds come by day to tear their prey, and the spirits of hell by night to plot murder. O Verkovsky! what have I done to you? Why efface from a mountaineer's heaven his most beautiful star, — liberty? Why? Because I have loved you too much, perhaps. I have sacrificed my love for you. You might have said simply, 'Ammalat, I need your life,' and I should have given it as simply as you had asked it. Like the son of Abraham, I should have lain down under the knife and died forgiving you.

"But to sell my liberty! To take me from Sultanetta! Oh, no, traitor!

"And he lives still!

"From time to time, like a dove flitting through the smoke of a fire, I see your beautiful face, my Sultanetta. Why, then, as once, does the sight not delight me? They would separate us, my darling, they would give you to another, and give me to the tomb. But it shall not be; I will come to you by a trail of blood. I will perform the frightful task imposed on me as the price of your possession and I shall possess you. Besides your friends, invite to our wedding the vultures and crows. Oh! I will set out a feast for all the guests. I will bestow a priceless kalim;[1] instead of a velvet cushion, I will place under the head of my bride the heart that I respected, that I loved almost as much as her own.

[1] Wedding-present.

"O innocent girl, you will be the cause of a horrible crime! Sweet creature, for you two friends will clutch each other's throats in an embrace of devilish rage. For you! for you! but is it indeed for you alone?

"I have twenty times heard Verkovsky say that it was cowardly to get rid of an enemy by a shot or a dagger-thrust.

"How strange these Europeans are! According to them, when an enemy has crushed your head with his heel, or your heart with his hands, you are to say: 'You have dishonored me; you have stripped my tree of life of its leaves; you have blighted the roses of my heart; let us fight! If I am the stronger, I shall kill you; if you are the stronger, you will kill me.'

"And they present their breasts to the traitor's ball or sword.

"Oh! it is not so with us, Verkovsky; but it was not enough that you should bind my hands, you would like to bind my conscience, too.

"Useless, wasted words!

"I have loaded my gun; my gun came from my father; my father had it from my grandfather. I have been told of many famous shots that it has sent home. True, never yet has it been fired in the dark, or in ambush. It has always breathed fire and spat death in battle, before the eyes of all, in the front rank; and it fought against noble warriors, worthy foes; it never had to avenge treachery or wrong. But now! Oh! tremble not, my hand! A charge of powder, a leaden ball, a flash, a report, an echo, and all is over.

"A charge of powder! what a little thing! Yet here it is in the hollow of my hand and barely does it cover it, yet it is enough to banish the soul from a man's body. Cursed be he that invented the gray powder that gives the hero's life to the coward's hand; that kills from afar the enemy off guard, that murders with a single look!

"So a single shot is to undo all my old ties and open my way to new ones. In the freshness of the mountains, on Sultanetta's bosom, my worn heart will regain its vigor. Like the swallow, I will make my nest in a foreign land and cast aside all past griefs, as one throws away an old garment tattered by brambles and thorns.

"But my conscience!

"Once it happened that I recognized in the enemies' ranks a man whom I had sworn to kill. I could have sent him a bullet without his knowing from where it came. I was ashamed. I turned my horse away and did not shoot. Yet I would pierce the heart on which I have rested as if it had been a brother's! He deceived me; but was it such a misfortune to believe in his friendship, however false?

"O that my tears could quench my rage, my thirst for vengeance, — that they could buy, could gain Sultanetta!

"But why does the dawn delay so long? Let it come! I will look upon the sun without blushing, and I will meet Verkovsky's eye without paling. My heart is pitiless. Treachery calls for treachery. I am resolved. Here is the day — it is the last.

"No. It was but a lightning flash."

And, to fortify himself with the courage which he felt he lacked, Ammalat Beg seized a bottle of wine that Sophyr Ali had brought him, and emptied it at one draught.

Then he fell back on his pillow; but it was of no avail; he could not sleep. A viper was devouring his heart.

Then he went to Sophyr Ali, who was asleep, and shook him roughly.

"Get up!" he cried; "it is light."

Sophyr Ali opened his eyes and regarded Ammalat with a yawn.

"Light! — on your cheeks; but it is the glow of wine that they reflect, and not of dawn."

"Get up, I tell you! The dead themselves must rise out of their graves to come to meet the one that I shall send them."

"What are you saying? Am I a dead man? You are going mad, by Allah! Ammalat Beg. Let the dead rise if it amuses them, let the forty imams come back with the dawn if it suits them; as for me, I am a live man that has not had enough sleep. Good-night!"

"You like to drink, Sophyr Ali. I am thirsty this morning; drink with me."

"Ah! that is another thing, and now your reason is returning. Pour out a glass full, pour a full horn. Allah! I am always ready to drink and to love."

"And to revenge yourself on an enemy, is it not so? Here's to the health of the devil, who turns friends into deadly enemies! Where I go, you follow, do you not, Sophyr Ali?"

"Ammalat, it is not only wine from the same bottle that we have drunk, but milk from the same mother. I will follow, should you build your nest on the top-most ledge of a Khunsack crag. However, a little advice —"

"No advice, Sophyr Ali; no reproaches, what is more. This is no time for either."

"You are right. Advice and reproaches would drown in wine like flies. It is no time for reproaches or advice, it is the time for sleep."

"For sleep, you say? There is no more sleep for me.

Have you examined the flint of my gun? Is it good? Did you renew the priming? it is not damp?"

"What is the matter, Ammalat? There is some mystery, some crime perhaps in your heart. Your eye is feverish, your face is livid; your words smell of blood."

"My deeds shall be more dreadful still, Sophyr Ali. Sultanetta is beautiful, — my Sultanetta! Is this a marriage song ringing in my ears? No, it is the roaring of demons, the wailing of jackals. Howl, wolves! weep demons! You are tired of waiting. Be quiet, you shall not wait long. More wine, Sophyr Ali! more wine! — and then, blood!"

Ammalat drained at a draught a second bottle, and fell dead drunk on his bed, muttering a few unintelligible words. Sophyr Ali undressed him, put him to bed, and watched at his pillow the remainder of the night, casting about in vain for an explanation of his words.

Finally, at break of day, he himself went to bed saying, —

"He was drunk"

XVI.

In the morning, before taking up his march, the captain who was on duty reported at the colonel's quarters.

After announcing that everything was in proper order in the regiment, he looked about, and approaching Verkovsky uneasily, he inquired: —

"Colonel, can I speak with you?"

"Certainly," answered Verkovsky, absently.

"But it is on a serious matter, colonel."

"A serious matter?"

"Yes."

"Speak, captain."

"We are quite alone?"

In turn, Verkovsky looked about.

"We are quite alone," said he.

"Colonel, what I have to tell you is of great importance, of very great importance."

"I am listening."

"Yesterday, at Bouinaky, a soldier of our regiment overheard a conversation between Ammalat and his nurse. He is a Tartar of Kasan who understands Caucasian Tartar perfectly. Well, he heard Ammalat's nurse, old Fatma, telling your prisoner that you and the chamkal wished to send him to Siberia. Ammalat was furious. He declared that he had already been forewarned by Ackmeth Khan of such an intention, but that he would kill you with his own hand first.

"Believing that he had misunderstood or that, if he had heard aright, you were in danger of death, the Tartar began yesterday to spy upon every movement of Ammalat's.

"In the evening Ammalat spoke with an unknown man, and, after greeting him, said,—

"'Tell the khan that to-morrow morning by sunrise all shall be over; let him be prepared; I shall see him soon.'"

"Is that all, captain?" asked Verkovsky.

"Don't you think that sufficient to disturb the men who love you, colonel? Listen to me: I have spent my life among the Tartars; he is a madman who puts faith in the best of them. The brother is not sure of his own head even at the moment when he rests it on his brother's shoulder."

"Jealousy is the cause of Ammalat's moodiness, captain. Cain left it as a heritage to mankind, and especially to those who dwell near Ararat. We have nothing to quarrel about, Ammalat and I. I have never done him aught but good, and I have no intention of doing him evil. Rest easy, then, captain. I have faith in your soldier's good intention, but not in his knowledge of the Tartar language. I am not so great a man that begs and khans seek to assassinate me, captain. I know Ammalat very well; he is violent, but he has a good heart."

"Don't deceive yourself, colonel; Ammalat is an Asiatic. Don't expect from him, therefore, either the virtues or the vices of a European. Here, it is not as with us; here, the word conceals the thought, the face masks the soul. A Tartar may seem an honest man on the surface; delve below it, and you will find vileness, fury, and ferocity."

"Experience may have given you the right to think thus, captain; but as for me, I have no reason to suspect Ammalat. What would he gain by killing me? I am his only hope. I was to have been dead by daylight; the sun is quite high above the horizon, and, as you see, I am still alive. I thank you nevertheless, captain; but do not suspect Ammalat. Now we must be on the march!"

The captain withdrew. The drums began to roll, and the regiment began its march.

The morning was clear and cool. The regiment looked like a long serpent with scales of steel, sometimes stretched at length at the bottom of a valley, sometimes crawling over the mountain.

Ammalat marched at the front, pale and sad. He hoped that the beating of the drum would drown the voice in his heart.

The colonel called him and said pleasantly, —

"I must scold you, Ammalat. You follow the teaching of Hafiz too strictly to the letter; wine is a good comrade, but a bad master. You have spent a bad night, Ammalat."

"Yes, a terrible night, colonel; Allah grant that I may never pass such another! I dreamed a great deal, — horrible dreams."

"Ammalat, Ammalat, we should not do what our religion forbids. Your conscience is no longer at peace."

"Happy is the man whose conscience has no enemy but wine!"

"What conscience do you mean, my friend? Every nation, every century has its own conscience: what yesterday was regarded as a crime, to-morrow will be glorified as a great deed."

"I presume, however," responded Ammalat, "that deceit, revenge, and murder were never regarded as virtues."

"I do not say that, although we live in a century in which success almost always carries its own absolution. The most conscientious men of this period do not hesitate to say and even to put in practice the proverb. 'The end justifies the means.' "

Ammalat cast a side glance at the colonel.

"Traitor!" he muttered to himself; "you talk indeed like a traitor."

Then, deeper down, within his inmost breast, within his heart, he added: —

"The hour is at hand!"

The colonel, unsuspicious, advanced beside the young man. At eight versts from Karakent they suddenly came in sight of the Caspian Sea.

Verkovsky became thoughtful.

"It is strange, Ammalat," said he, "I cannot look upon your sad sea, your wild country, full of diseases, and of men worse than the diseases, without a pang of the heart and a saddening of soul. I hate war with invisible enemies. I hate to serve with comrades who are seldom our friends. I serve my country with love, the emperor with loyalty; in order to perform my military duties, I deny myself all the joys of life; my mind is petrified from inaction, my heart interred in solitude. I have torn myself away from everything, even from my heart's beloved. What recompense have I received? A secondary rank. When will the hour arrive in which I may rush into the arms of my betrothed? How long will it be before, tired of service, I shall rest in my home on the banks of the Dnieper? At last I have my leave in my pocket. In five days I shall be at Georgievsk;

yet it is strange, but I approach her in vain; it always seems as if the Libyan desert, a sea of ice, an eternity as dark and infinite as that of the tomb, lay between us. Oh! my heart, my poor heart!"

Verkovsky became silent; he was weeping.

His horse, feeling his bridle abandoned, quickened his pace, and Ammalat and he outstripped the regiment.

He delivered himself into the hands of his murderer.

But, at sight of his tears, at the sound of his stifled sobs, pity stole into Ammalat's heart, as a ray of sunlight penetrates a gloomy cave.

He looked upon the grief of him who had so long been his friend, and he said to himself,—

"No, it is impossible for a man to dissemble to such an extent."

But, as if ashamed of his momentary weakness, Verkovsky raised his head, and trying to smile, he said,—

"Be ready, Ammalat, you are to go with me."

At these fatal words, every good impulse remaining in Ammalat's heart was crushed.

The thought of the agreement between the colonel and the chamkal presented itself to his mind, and the path of eternal exile unfolded before him.

"With you?" he said, his lips quivering with anger, "with you into Russia? If you are going there, why not?"

And he burst into a laugh so strange that it sounded like the grinding of teeth, and, whipping up his horse, he bounded ahead.

He must have time to get his gun ready.

Then he turned his horse, bore down upon the colonel and rode past him; then he began to circle about him like an eagle with its prey.

At each round he became paler, more furious, more

threatening. It seemed to him that the breath of a demon was hissing in his ear, and saying, —

"Kill! kill! kill!"

All this while, the colonel, suspecting nothing, looked smilingly on at Ammalat's evolutions, thinking that, after the fashion of the Asiatics, he wished him to admire his adroitness in executing the whim.

He saw him bring his gun to his shoulder and thinking that he was continuing the sport, the colonel lifted his helmet from his head and shouted, —

"Into my fouraska! into my fouraska! I will throw it up for you."

"No," said Ammalat Beg, "into your heart!"

And at ten paces from the colonel, he fired.

The colonel uttered not a sound, not a sigh, as he fell.

The ball had pierced his heart, as Ammalat had intended.

Ammalat's horse, swept onward in his course, stopped before the dead body, falling back on his haunches.

Ammalat leaped to the ground, and stood leaning on his smoking gun, as if he would prove to himself that he was insensible to that dead gaze, and cool in the presence of the blood which streamed from the wound.

What was passing just then in the heart of the assassin? God alone knows.

Sophyr Ali came up and flung himself on his knees beside the dead man.

He bent over the lips; the lips were still.

"He is dead!" cried Sophyr Ali, in dismay, as he stared at Ammalat.

"Is he quite dead?" said the latter, as if he were awakening from a heavy sleep. "In that case, so much the better; for his death is my happiness."

"Your happiness!" cried Sophyr Ali; "yours, the

murderer of your benefactor! The day when you will find happiness is the day on which the whole world shall renounce God and worship the devil."

"Sophyr Ali," said Ammalat, roughly, "remember that you are my servant, and not my judge."

And, springing upon his horse, he said, —

"Follow me!"

"May remorse alone follow you like a spectre, not I. Do what you will, turn out as you may, from this day we are nothing more to each other, and I renounce you for my brother. Farewell, Cain!"

At this response from Sophyr Ali, Ammalat uttered a groan, and, signing to his noukars to follow him, he darted as swiftly as an arrow into the mountains. Ten minutes later, the head of the Russian column halted before its dead colonel.

XVII.

AMMALAT wandered three days in the mountains of Daghestan.

Although he was among the conquered villages, he felt secure, the mountaineers in spite of their submission keeping their sympathies for the enemies of the Russians.

But, beyond the reach of danger, he was not beyond the reach of remorse, and Sophyr Ali's curse clung to him with an iron grasp. Neither his heart nor his brain essayed to excuse his crime, now that it was committed. He had always before him that final moment of the murder when, in the midst of the smoke enveloping both assassin and victim, the colonel had fallen from his horse. It was an Asiatic who committed the first crime, who became the first traitor, and the tradition of everlasting remorse was born at the foot of Ararat.

Yet his task was not ended with the murder; it remained for him to perform a ghastlier deed than that.

"Do not show yourself in Khunsack without the head of Verkovsky," Ackmeth Khan had said; and, as if no degree of crime was to be spared him after his first, he must now secure the head.

Among the Orientals, an enemy is not regarded as really dead until he is decapitated. Vengeance is not complete unless his adversary's head is in the hands of the avenger.

Not daring to discover his intention to his noukars, upon whose courage on such an occasion he knew that he could not rely, he resolved to return alone to Derbend across the mountain.

And, indeed, none of his men would have hesitated to commit on the battlefield an act which every mountaineer regards as a matter of course in war; but none of them would have dared to enter a cemetery at night and violate a tomb.

However, this is what remained for Ammalat to do.

The night was dark when the young man emerged from the hollow cave a half-verst distant from the fortress of Marienkale, which serves as a citadel for Derbend. He tied his horse to a tree at the top of the hill from which Yermolof, yet a lieutenant, had stormed Derbend. A hundred paces from this hill lay the Russian cemetery.

But, in the total darkness, how was he to find the new grave of Verkovsky?

The sky was overcast and the clouds hovering over the earth seemed to rest on the mountains; the wind sweeping from the valleys seemed, like a night-bird, to beat the branches of the trees with its wings.

Ammalat shuddered as he entered this realm of the dead, whose funereal repose he had come to disturb.

He listened.

The sea roared as it broke upon its shore; around him re-echoed the howling of the wolves and jackals whose comrade he had become. Then, suddenly, every sound ceased, save that eternal, mournful soughing of the wind, which seemed like the wailing of the spirits of the dead.

How many times on just such a night had he waked with Verkovsky! What had become of that intelligent soul, who at such times had explained to him all nature's mysteries, in that unknown region whither he had hurled him?

At such times he used to listen to him, lying near him or

leaning on his arm. And now, after having snatched life from the body, behold, a despoiler of tombs, he was coming to snatch the head from the grave!

"Human terrors!" murmured Ammalat, wiping his forehead that streamed with perspiration, "what are you doing now in a heart where nothing human remains? Away! away! What! I have taken a man's life and now fear to take the head from the body, when that head means a treasure for me? Truly, I am mad! Are not the dead without feeling?"

With a trembling hand Ammalat lighted some dry sticks, and by their feeble and flickering light, he began to search for the colonel's grave. Some newly turned earth and a cross on which was to be read the name of Verkovsky, indicated the last resting-place of him whom he had so often called brother. He uprooted the cross and began to open the grave.

The task was neither long nor difficult. In the Orient, interments are made almost on a level with the ground.

Ammalat's poniard very soon struck the lid of the coffin.

By a last effort the lid was raised.

In the ruddy light of the burning branches he was obliged to take a last look at the body.

The torture was terrible, supreme, unlike any torment that human justice could have devised. While bending over the body, Ammalat, more livid than the corpse itself, seemed for an instant as if turned into stone. What had he come there to do? How and why was he there? Not a throb of his suspended heart, not a fibre of his arrested brain could have made answer; the odor of the dead enveloped him, a vapor of death dimmed his sight.

"Yet it must be ended!" he murmured, trying to draw himself from his stupor by the sound of his own words.

But not vanity, nor revenge, nor love, nor any feeling whose frenzy had driven him to commit his first crime was sustaining him now in the accomplishment of his second. The second was more than a crime, it was sacrilege.

At last, he set his poniard against the neck which he must cut, cast his torch far behind him that he might conceal his infamous task from himself under the cover of darkness, and, after a few futile efforts, he felt with horror that he had achieved his end.

The head was severed from the body.

He took it, and, with an indefinable feeling of anguish and disgust, he threw it into a sack which he had brought for the purpose.

Until then, he had felt master of himself; but, in that moment, when he understood that the more cowardly of his two deeds was accomplished; when there hung from his arm that head which he thought to exchange for happiness; when he was forced to drag his feet from that soft and sliding earth, the earth of the tomb in which he was standing up to his knees; when, in shaking off the dust of the dead, his foot slipped on the pebbles and he fell back into the open grave, as if the corpse in its turn would not let him go, — ah! then all his presence of mind deserted him. It seemed to him that he was going mad.

The lighted sticks which he had flung behind him had set fire to the grass scorched by the burning sun of June. He had forgotten how the flame came to be there. For him it was that of hell. It seemed to him as if the spirits of darkness, laughing and crying, were leaping about him. He himself began to weep, began to laugh, and then with a low moan in which were blended his laughter and tears, he fled without looking behind him.

At last, on the hill he found his horse, mounted him, spurred him on into the mountains unheeding of rocks and precipices, taking every bush that caught him for the staying hand of the corpse, and the cries of the jackals and hyenas for the last death-rattle of his benefactor, twice murdered by him.

He arrived at Khunsack on the evening of the second day.

Trembling with impatience, he leaped down from his horse, and untied from his saddle-bow the accursed sack.

He ascended the well-known flight of steps and passed through the first rooms.

They were crowded with mountaineers in war costume. Some walked about wearing breastplates of mail, others were talking, lying side by side on their bourkas.

All spoke in low tones, — those, at least, who spoke, for the greater number maintained a gloomy silence.

The frowning brows, the darkened faces indicated that they were depressed by sad tidings at Khunsack.

Noukars ran hither and thither; all knew Ammalat and yet none of them questioned him. No one appeared to notice him.

Near the door of Ackmeth Khan's room stood Soukay Khan, his second son. He was weeping bitterly.

"What does this mean?" demanded Ammalat, with forebodings of ill. "You, who are called the child without tears, are now weeping?"

Soukay Khan, without answering a word, pointed to the door of the room.

Ammalat entered.

There a terrible spectacle was presented.

In the centre of the room, on a mattress covered over with a rug, lay Ackmeth Khan, already disfigured by the touch of death. From time to time his breast heaved, but it was attended by painful effort.

He was just entering on that last agonizing struggle awaiting man at the entrance to the tomb.

His wife and daughter were on their knees before him, weeping. His eldest son, Montzale Khan, crouched motionless at his feet, his head buried in his hands.

At a little distance from the dying man several women and favorite noukars were weeping.

But, full of the terrible thought burning within him, Ammalat approached the khan, and, he alone standing in the midst of these stricken people, said,—

"Good day, khan! I bring you a present which might bring a dead man to life. Prepare the wedding; here is Sultanetta's wedding-gift."

And with these words he threw the colonel's head at the khan's feet.

Ammalat's voice had seemed to rouse the dying man. He raised himself to see the present which the young beg had brought him. Verkovsky's severed head was at his feet.

A shudder passed through his frame.

"May he eat out his own heart," said he, "who brings such a sight to the eyes of a dying man!"

Then, raising himself with a last effort, and lifting both hands to heaven, the khan said,—

"Allah be my witness that I pardon all my enemies; but you, you, Ammalat, I curse you!"

And he fell back dead on his cushions.

The wife of Ackmeth Khan had stared with deep-seated terror at what had just passed. But, when she saw her husband dead, believing that the sight of Ammalat and his fatal gift had hastened his death, with eyes aflame she pointed to the dead man and cried, —

"Messenger of hell! look, that is your work. Without you my husband would never have dreamed of setting Avarie in revolt against the Russians; without you, he would at this moment be well and at peace. But, for you and through you, while going to rouse the begs, he fell from the height of a rock; and you, wretch! you, traitor! you, murderer! instead of coming to soften his agony and ease his death, come like a wild beast and throw amid the phantoms around the bed of a dying man, that ghastly thing, that severed head! And whose head? Your defender's, your friend's, your benefactor's!"

"But it was the khan's will!" cried Ammalat, thunderstruck.

"Don't accuse the dead. Don't stain with useless blood the body of one who cannot defend himself," returned the widow more and more exasperated, — "you, who fear not to come and ask the daughter in marriage at her father's death-bed, who expect to receive man's reward while obtaining the curse of God. Sacrilege and infamy! I vow by the tomb of my ancestors, by the swords of my sons, by the honor of my daughter, that you shall never be my son-in-law, nor my guest. Out of my house, traitor!"

Ammalat uttered a cry.

"Go!" added the widow; "I have sons whom you could strangle with an embrace; I have a daughter whom you could poison with a look. Hide yourself in the caves of our mountains; there teach the tigers to devour each other. Go! and know one thing, my door shall never be opened to an assassin."

Ammalat seemed stricken by a thunderbolt.

All that the low voice of conscience had already said was repeated aloud and with cruelty. He knew not where to look. On the floor was Verkovsky's head; on the bed was Ackmeth's body; before him, the widow — the curse!

Yet Sultanetta's eyes, drowned in tears, shone like two stars through a cloud.

He approached her saying, —

"Sultanetta, that I did it all for you, you know well, and I am losing you. If fate wills, it must be; but only tell me if you, too, hate me; if you, too, spurn me?"

Sultanetta lifted her welling eyes to the one she had so loved; but at the sight of Ammalat's face, pale and spotted with blood, she hid her eyes with one hand, and with the other pointing alternately to her father's body and the colonel's head, she said firmly, —

"Farewell, Ammalat. I pity you, but never will I be yours."

And, overcome by her struggle, she fell fainting beside the body of her father.

The native pride of Ammalat surged back to his heart with his blood.

"Ah! thus am I received here," said he, casting a look of contempt toward the two women; "thus are oaths fulfilled in the house of Ackmeth Khan! Ah! I am satisfied, and my eyes see clearly, at last! I was indeed mad to stake my happiness on the heart of a fickle girl, and I have been patient indeed in listening to the imprecations of an old woman. In dying, Ackmeth Khan took with him the honor and the hospitality of his house. Make way! I go."

Throwing a look of defiance at the khan's sons, the noukars and cavaliers who, attracted by the disturbance, were crowding into the room, he advanced toward them, his hand on the hilt of his kandjiar, as if to invite them to combat.

But all stood aside, avoiding rather than fearing him, and not a word more was addressed to him, either in the chamber of the dead or while passing through the other rooms.

On the steps he found his noukars, and below, his horse.

He sprang into the saddle without saying a word, left the palace at a walk, went slowly through the streets of Khunsack; then, from the height whence he had first seen the khan's house, he gave it a last look.

His heart was full of bitterness, his eyes were charged with blood; offended pride was grappling its hooks of steel into the depths of his heart.

In lowering wrath, he cast a last look upon that house where he had known and lost all the pleasures of the world.

He tried to speak; he tried to pronounce the name of Sultanetta; he tried to accuse; he tried to curse.

He could not utter a single word, a mountain of lead seemed to have fallen upon him.

Finally, as a last expedient he tried to weep; it seemed to him that this enormous weight oppressing him must be of tears; it seemed to him that a tear, a single one, would reconcile him with human kind and implore God's pardon.

"One tear! one tear! only one tear!" he cried.

All was useless; his eyes remained dry, burning, arid. Moreover, one must love and be loved in order to shed tears, and Ammalat, like Satan, hated and was hated.

The days, the months, the years rolled by.

Where was Verkovsky's assassin? What had become of him?

No one knew.

It was rumored indeed that he was among the Tchetchens, where his kounack Nephtali had been unable to deny him hospitality. The curse of the dying Ackmeth Khan was said to have bereft him of everything: beauty, health, courage even.

But who could confirm it?

At last, little by little, Ammalat was forgotten; but the memory of his treachery is to-day still fresh and vivid among Russians and Tartars.

EPILOGUE.

In 1828, the fortress of Anapa was beleaguered by land and sea, by the fleets and armies of Russia.

Every morning a new battery, sprung up in the night, thundered nearer the town.

The Turkish garrison, backed by the mountaineers forever at war with Russia, bravely held their ground.

On the south side of the town the Russians at last succeeding in effecting a breach.

The wall was crumbling under their balls; but its thickness made the work a slow and laborious task.

From time to time — especially during the intense heat of the day — the reddened cannon and the wearied gunners were accorded a respite of an hour or two.

During one of these resting spells, while the gunners were sleeping, suddenly, from the top of the wall, a horseman on a white horse was seen descending, supported by ropes passed under the animal's stomach.

Scarcely had he touched the ground, when the ropes were withdrawn over the top of the wall, the horseman cleared the fosse at a leap, and, setting his horse at a gallop, passed like a streak of light between batteries and soldiers.

A few shots pursued him, but without effect; he disappeared in the forest.

They had barely caught sight of him; no one dreamed of following.

Very soon their minds were distracted by the renewed cannonading, and all forgot the horseman.

Before night the breach had become practicable; the Russians were preparing for the onset, when suddenly, from the side next the forest, they were attacked by mountaineers.

The terrible cry, "Allah il Allah!" was answered from the walls of Anapa.

But the Russians turned their guns on these unlooked-for assailants and soon scattered the mountaineers, who took to flight, leaving their dead and wounded on the battle-field, and howling, "Giaours! giaours!"

But, from the beginning of this affair, and up to the moment when the battle-field was cleared, the Russians could see in front of them a Circassian mounted on a white horse held at a walk, and moving back and forth before the Russian batteries, unmindful alike of the balls and bullets that were raining around him.

The impassiveness, and, above all, the invulnerability of the mountaineer rendered the gunners furious. The balls, ripping the earth around him, dashed it under his horse's feet. The horse reared and plunged, but his rider kept the frightened creature to his course, soothing him with his hand, and apparently heedless of the danger enveloping him on every side.

"The horse for me and twenty-five roubles for you," said an officer of artillery to the artillery-man of his battery, "if you bring down that knave."

The artillery-man looked up.

"I have aimed at him three times already," said he, "and it must be that the devil himself is sitting that horse; but, captain," he continued, "you may load my gun with my own head for the next shot, if I miss him this time."

And, having pointed his cannon with especial care, he took the match from his comrade's hand and fired it himself.

For an instant, it was impossible to distinguish anything; but soon the smoke was dissipated and they saw the frightened horse dragging his master's body, whose foot was caught in the stirrup.

"Hit! dead!" cried the soldiers.

The young officer lifted his helmet, made the sign of the cross, and leaped over the battery to catch the horse, which was a fine animal, born, as well as they could judge, in Khorassan.

He was very soon caught. The animal kept moving in the same circle, dragging the mountaineer's body.

The ball had taken off an arm of the latter near the shoulder; but he was still breathing.

The young officer summoned four gunners and had the dying man carried to his own tent.

He himself went for the surgeon.

But, upon examining the frightful wound, the surgeon declared that the shoulder would have to be disjointed, and that the man would die under the operation.

It was better, then, to let him die quietly from his wound than to cause him to die sooner and more painfully.

The surgeon ordered a refreshing drink, the only relief that he could give the sufferer.

The officer sat alone in his tent beside his guest in the pangs of death, having no one near him but a Tartar interpreter, whom he could summon in case of returning consciousness, when the dying man, whom he easily recognized as a chief, might have some last request to make.

Towards one o'clock in the morning, the wounded man

seemed troubled, often sighing, as if some vision were taking part in his death-struggle.

The young officer rose, held the lantern close to the face of the injured man, who had not yet regained consciousness, and regarded him more attentively than he had yet done.

The expression of the man's countenance was sad; deep wrinkles furrowed his brow and disfigured a face that must have been beautiful before having been ploughed by the unruly passions of which it bore trace. It was easy to see, however, that its wan look proceeded rather from the sorrows of life than from the painful seizure of death.

His breathing became more and more labored.

With his remaining hand, he seemed to be striving to thrust back some vengeful apparition. At last, his speech found utterance, and, after a few unintelligible words, the officer and the interpreter succeeded in grasping these: —

"Blood! forever blood!" murmured the mutilated man looking at his remaining hand, the right hand. "Why have you covered me with his blood-stained garment? Am I not already wading in blood? Do not drag me in that direction, back to life. Life is hell! The grave is so quiet, and so cool! — " Again he fainted, and the words died on his lips.

The officer asked the interpreter for some water, dipped his hand in the glass, and with his fingers sprinkled the face of the dying one.

The latter quivered, opened his eyes, shook his head as if to avoid the enveloping shadow of death, and then, by the glimmering light of the lantern which the interpreter was holding, he perceived the captain.

From being vague, his gaze became fixed and wild.

He stared at the officer, tried to rise on the missing arm, fell back, and rose on the other.

His hair stood on end, the perspiration rolled from his brow, his pale face became livid, his countenance little by little assumed an expression of profoundest terror.

"Your name?" he said in a shaking voice, that no longer held anything of human semblance. "Who are you? Are you a messenger from the tomb? Tell me! speak! answer!"

"My name is Verkovsky," responded the young man, briefly.

These words, very simple in themselves, produced the effect of a kandjiar-thrust in the wounded man's heart. He shrieked, shuddered, and fell back on his pillow.

"This man was undoubtedly a great sinner," said the young officer, sadly, addressing himself to the interpreter.

"Or a great traitor," the latter added; "he must be, or he must have been,— for he is dead,— some Russian deserter. I have never heard a mountaineer speak our tongue with such purity. Let us look at his weapons; we shall there find, perhaps, some inscription. The armorers of Kouba, Andrev, and Koubatche often add to their own name the name of the one for whom the weapon is made."

And, drawing the kandjiar from the dead man's girdle, he began to examine the blade.

This inscription was engraved in gold on the burnished steel.

"*Be slow to offend, and quick to avenge.*"

The interpreter translated it for the young officer.

"Yes, that is a maxim of these brigands," said the latter. "My poor brother, the colonel, fell a victim of one of these wretches."

The young man brushed away a tear. Then, to the interpreter he continued: —

"Now examine the sheath."

The interpreter detached the sheath from the dead man's girdle, and found engraved thereon these words in the Tartar character: —

"*I was made for Ammalat Beg.*"

Printed in the United States
44575LVS00001B/17